Painted Rocks

A Novel

By Kimberly Ann Freel

Country Messenger Press Publishing Group, LLC
Oroville, Washington

All inquiries should be addressed to:
CMPPG, LLC
PO BOX 1165
Oroville, WA 98844

Painted Rocks may be ordered from CMPPG, LLC at the above address and at cmppg.com
Painted Rocks is also available on Amazon.com

Contact publisher for Distributor information.

email: cmppg@cmppg.com
website: cmppg.com

ISBN 0-9619407-9-4

Dedication

The author wishes to thank Richard Merriman for his invaluable guidance in the editing of this debut novel.

To my family, too numerous to mention, and so incredibly supportive that I can't imagine realizing this dream without any of them.

To Christopher, who by presenting me with a laptop computer, opened up the vault of my imagination, for which I will be forever grateful.

And, finally, to my children, Livia, Emma, and Zander who have taught me that love has no bounds or limitations.

Authors Note:

A city-dwelling friend of mine once said on a visit to the Okanogan that if I could make my fortune as an author, I could find my way out of here, back to a city, back to what he considered a normal life. I pondered his suggestion, but only briefly. I had lived in the city, two cities, actually. I loved the culture, the lights, the excitement, and the hustle. Apart from those things, I was secretly homesick.

I spent my entire childhood and adolescence trying to leave here. But the longer I spent away, the more I was drawn back. The unspoiled beauty and simplicity of this life allow me to live peacefully with my family and to write without distraction or hesitation.

My friend couldn't possibly understand that people live this life by choice, not circumstance. Many people of the Okanogan have lived the urban life, only to return, willingly and happily. We couldn't fathom leaving here even with a windfall in hand.

Besides, as I reminded my urban friend, sometimes the most interesting stories begin in the remotest of places. It is with that in mind that I begin this, my very first novel.

Foreword:

Many miles through Washington State, up the mighty Columbia River just shy of the Canadian border, lies the mouth of the Okanogan River. The Okanogan River forms the valley that makes its way North through a series of tiny towns to its origin in British Columbia.

The towns are divided by miles and miles of sage brush and spotty pine trees. Okanogan County is huge in land mass, roughly the size of the State of Connecticut. It is, however, the least densely populated county in the State. Coyotes and rattlesnakes far outnumber humans.

Orchards and small family farms are randomly plotted around the valley, still a common way to make a living. A few of the farms of the county are immaculate. Every piece of haying equipment has a proper place and shelter. Every fence is maintained. The barns and houses are painted every other year and they match one another.

The flowerbeds are plentiful and neatly weeded. Even the horses and cattle look content, well fed and harmonious, as if they are painted into the pastoral scene, more decoration than money-making stock. And if the family owns more than two cars, the extras are kept carefully out of sight of the road.

More commonly, however, the properties of this rural county are a helter-skelter combination of pasture, sage brush, mismatched outbuildings, yards scattered with toddler pools and tacky lawn ornaments, all surrounding aging mobile homes. Quite a few are further decorated with automobiles of various makes and models, none of which actually run, but provide their owners with parts and possibilities.

The Rinker property was just such a place. Much to the horror of their neater neighbors, the Rinkers could have easily opened a junkyard with the menagerie of cars and trucks they had accumulated. Grandpa August Rinker had started the collection with good intentions—he had a beat-up Ford Fairlane that could have looked like a million bucks with some straighter parts, elbow grease, and his knowledge of American automobiles.

When he ran across a second Fairlane in the North County that could be used for parts, he jumped at the chance to hook a chain up to the front bumper and mosey the car down the highway. This one, of course, had been stripped of its engine and much of the tranny, so August Rinker set out to find another Ford (or two) that could provide him with the innards for his original beloved Fairlane.

Trouble was, Grandpa August's vast knowledge of cars had to do more with what had been manufactured in what year and who had made it. He really knew nothing about taking them apart and putting them back together. He knew even less about the magic that made them go from gleaming hunks of metal to useful vehicles.

He was, in a sense, just a collector. The result was a colorful line-up of rusty automobiles and a less-than-artful arrangement of parts that had been removed from their vehicles and never relocated.

An aerial photographer had come around one year with sample prints of the property and nifty frames. Nirval Rinker, grandson of August, and by inheritance the proud owner, was so taken with the glittering, multihued patchwork that was his fifteen acres that he bought all the prints the man brought with him. He also ordered enough to make Christmas gifts for his six uncles and two aunts and all of the lucky Rinker cousins.

It was on a dusty gravel road just a quarter mile from the industrious Rinkers, under a blazing summer sun, that this remarkable journey begins.

Part One

Chapter One

Thirteen year-old Sunny Moss was fit to be tied. The summer sun was intense enough to burn her scalp right through the part in her hair. Sunny could feel the instant sunburn. Yet she continued her march to her friend Crystal's house. She figured that if she stomped the gravel hard enough it might ease some of the frustration she was feeling. Besides the dry heat was sort of soothing, absorbing the moisture of her furious tears.

She and her Mom had gotten in another fight. They might have worked it out on their own, but her Dad, tipsy *again* after a day at the lake, had walked in the back door at just the wrong time.

In the laundry room, among the carefully arranged piles of clothes, he had found his daughter and his wife locked into battle-mode. Patty Moss' face and neck were beet red with irritation. Sunny was calling her mother all kinds of filthy names. He wasn't sure what had Sunny fired up, but when Patty tried to leave the room to settle her own emotions, Sunny grabbed her by the upper arms and told her to pay attention.

Gus Moss had seen enough in just a few seconds to decide that he needed to intervene. Sunny may have had her reasons, but he also knew that Patty would never strike back or yell at her daughter. Patty's own mother was a self-righteous woman who had never hesitated to verbally or physically correct her two daughters. Patty may have mouthed off to Gus more than a few times—more than he cared to remember, actually. But she never had raised hand, or voice, to stubborn, difficult Sunny or her brother, Avery.

In Patty's eyes, this made her a much better mother than Margaret Smith had ever been. She cared enough about her kids to show infallible self-control, regardless of their behavior.

In Sunny's eyes, this meant that she didn't care enough to pay attention to her. No matter how much she belittled and physically threatened her mother, Patty just didn't feel strongly enough about her and her problems to react. Sunny had always needed more attention than other children and she simply could not get it from her mother—good or bad.

Sunny had told them both to "go to Hell" on her way out the door. Then she made a quick exit before her Dad could smack her a good one.

Her parents just did not understand her at all. Sunny didn't know consciously that she was looking for punishment, just attention of any kind, positive or negative. She just knew that she felt ignored, frustrated.

She had gotten upset with her mom in the first place because Patty refused to take her town that evening for a movie. She didn't have time, she said. Besides, Sunny was grounded because she hadn't taken out the garbage like she'd been asked to do.

They treated her like a slave. They never did anything

nice for her. Sunny was tired of them. Period. Why couldn't she just have new parents?

She needed Crystal right now. Her best friend, Crystal Rinker, always understood her. She would sympathize with Sunny and then Sunny would hide out with her for a while. She would do anything rather than going home right then.

Little did Sunny know that her anger and resentment were about to culminate in an event that would change her life forever. She was about to lose her virginity in a ridiculously hot Ford Fairlane with the help of Crystal's big brother Duwayne and a bottle of whiskey.

Sunny was looking for her best friend when she got to the Rinkers, but Crystal had gone out to Riverside to ride horses with another friend of theirs, and the only one home was Duwayne.

Since she'd just as soon prefer to hang out with him than go home to her pathetic mom and dad, she watched with little trepidation as Duwayne swiped a bottle of whiskey from under the kitchen sink and prompted her to follow him out the door of the trailer to the Rinker junkyard.

She thought she might get pleasantly drunk. This was something she hadn't tried before. It was time to show some chin, to stage a minor sort of rebellion. To show her parents that she wasn't to be pushed around. It would definitely ruffle their feathers if she got drunk before she came home.

What she didn't plan for was getting physical with Duwayne. After all, he was Crystal's oldest brother—cute in a rough sort of way, but completely too old for her.

When Duwayne started to kiss her, she was a bit taken

3

aback, but didn't think it could do any harm. It was when he practically stuck his tongue down her throat that she pushed him away.

"What's the matter, Sunny? Don't you like playing mouth hockey with aliquor puck?" His drunken, lazy smile made her heart race. He had always had this effect on her!

She feigned disgust, "Gross, Duwayne. If I was planning on a make-out session, I wouldn't have come to see Crystal. I would have come to *you* right away." He had to *know* that it wasn't that easy, that *she* wasn't that easy!

"What did you *think* you were gonna do in the back seat of a beat-up car with me? Get drunk? I wanted us to have some privacy so I could show you some things that all skinny little runts like you should know. After all, I wouldn't want some stupid, inexperienced boy making mistakes with you on your first time around. I wouldn't want that for my sister either."

"How would you know this is the first time?" Surely Crystal wouldn't have told him any of her deep, dark secrets, would she?

"You don't think I can hear you and my lame little sister through the thin walls of the trailer? The way you titter and giggle all hours of the night, I'd have to be deaf to not know all your stupid secrets. Like, for instance, I know that you let Tommy Britt French-kiss you on the hill behind the football field. It would really suck for you if you let a loser like him get any further."

Embarrassment—warmth and redness creeping up her fair neck—came over her in waves. Crystal was her best friend. They had talked about their most personal feelings and experiences, including the small crush that she had had on Duwayne since they were little. But she had a wealth of experience hiding her feelings from everyone, including her parents. She decided she would play this tough.

"Tommy at least knows how to kiss without tangling up with my tonsils. I thought you, of all people, would be a better kisser. Besides, if you're trying to get down my pants, you might try being less of a smartass." 'That'll fix his attitude,' she thought.

Duwayne reddened, and then, feeling just a little chastened and a lot horny, he decided to take a different approach. After all, like his Grandpa August and his proud Daddy, he was a smart guy, and he knew how to get what he wanted. And what he wanted at that particular moment was a piece of hot, naïve little Sunny.

"Listen. I know you came all of the way over here to avoid letting your parents yell at you and the last thing I want to do is tick you off. I just want to show you how to feel good." He smiled that sleazy, confoundingly charming smile again and his brown eyes took on an expectant glaze.

By now the effects of the alcohol and the hot car were making her head swim. What Duwayne misread about Sunny was that her naivete did not equal stupidity. Sure she *was* awfully young, but she needed, deep down in her gut, to feel wanted by somebody, anybody. Duwayne would have to do. Besides, he would never actually hurt her.

Duwayne was nineteen and a man of considerable experience, or so he told her. He was the perfect one to shed her of her inhibitions and her chastity. After all, hadn't they known each other since Sunny was a snot-nosed two-year-old in his own mama's daycare?

"Okay, Duwayne. I'll let you show me some things. But you have to stop if I tell you to."

Then she let her mind go to a liquor-induced fog. She wrapped her prepubescent body around the boy she'd known all her life. Did it occur to her that she might be letting go of something precious that she could never get back? Well, the back of her mind still functioned on that level, but the fervent attention she was getting was filling a void she couldn't manage to fill at home. She'd had so little of actually feeling wanted by her family.

The slightly painful, unpleasant moment she knew she couldn't turn back from the decision she'd made, Sunny shed a single tear and then retreated behind the tough façade she'd erected for most of her thirteen years. But, oh, how she wept inside for the innocence she had just thrown hastily away.

Chapter Two

Sunny felt a brush against her arm as she walked home; and without thinking, she swiped at it and got stung by a bee. Knowing that her dad was deathly allergic to bee stings, she momentarily panicked. What if she had a reaction and swelled up and couldn't breathe and couldn't get home? Her dad would find her dead in the middle of the road. They would be sorry then, wouldn't they?

She figured the best she could do was keep going. So she continued to saunter down the sagebrush-lined road, trying to ignore the smarting sting. At the dirt road leading from their neighbor's place across the main road to their hay barn, a skinny, black tomcat darted out into her path. At sighting her, he stopped, flicked his tail in the air and looked imploringly at her as if she were encroaching on his mousing territory.

Sunny stared him down, and he decided to slink away into the brush. Trouble was, he took the wrong path. He was officially 'a black cat crossing her path.' Lord! And she was definitely superstitious. Between the black cat and the bee-sting, Sunny had to wonder whether her 'third bad thing' was going to happen on the way home or when she got there.

She knew the answer as soon as she walked through the front door. Her older brother, Avery, was bellied up to the kitchen bar, swigging a Bud and making her mom laugh. For whatever reason, his animated gesturing and the story he told was annoying her dad. The expression on Gus' face could only spell trouble.

Gaylord "Gus" Moss sat in his recliner glaring at his stepson. Sunny could tell he was still in a foul mood from their earlier argument. He had always been jealous of Patty Moss' eldest child. He thought she'd spoiled him from the get-go and she still paid too much attention to the overgrown mutt of a young man he'd become.

Gus had met Patty when she was bartending at "The Club," the local watering hole. She had been such a hot little number with her bombshell blonde hair and the "Patricia" stretched tightly across her left breast. He practically broke out in a sweat every time she'd bend over the dishwasher in her short denim skirt. He finally got the courage to ask her out his third time there, but only *after* his fifth Budweiser.

Avery's biological dad had also been a bar-hopping, beer-swilling, lady-killing type, though much younger than Gus. Patty should have known better than to give Gus the time of day. But there was a quiet shyness about Gus that intrigued her. She'd also learned from the grill cook that Gus was gainfully employed by the Okanogan County Public Works Department. That he had a job and kept it was a trait that a poor, unwed, hard-working mother from the South County valued very much.

Gus was, at the time, thirty-two years old. He was, in

Patty's twenty-three-year-old eyes, mature and stable—two characteristics that would benefit her and her fatherless son. Never mind that Gus barely tolerated Avery, whose five-year-old body and keen mind made him more energetic and troublesome than the average kid. Gus would adapt and Avery would charm him like he did everybody else.

Patty had found herself a marrying kind of man and Gus was in love with her bright smile and shapely body, which she offered to him with great regularity. He had been a bachelor long enough and Patty, as far as he could see, was the best that Okanogan County had to offer.

They married at the courthouse with Avery, Patty's mother Margaret, and Gus' bar buddy, Frank, as their witnesses. Two years later they birthed a baby girl, Sunny. Patty was happy with her 60's era, three-bedroom, split-level home and her two active children. It sure beat bartending. She probably would have seen more of her husband if she *had* been working at The Club. Gus liked his beer and his friends, and he hadn't been about to give that up.

As long as he provided the necessities for her and her children, Patty was content, if not blissfully in love. Gus loved that his wife kept his home so nice and still met his needs in the bedroom. She even stopped nagging him about his time at the bar after about a year of arguing.

Avery, on the other hand, had always been and would always be his mom's knight in shining armor. He had thought Gus worthless from the beginning, so he set about misbehaving in about every way possible. He had hoped his mom would change her mind about marrying him when he cut the lace fringe off her knee-length wedding dress—he had been pretending to be an Arabian prince and it made nice, soft stuffing for his turban (which he fashioned out of Gus' favorite silk shirt.)

No such luck—she had laughed at Avery's originality and married Gus anyway, in a different dress. Avery hadn't given up his shenanigans where Gus was concerned, though. He was intelligent enough to make his hijinks look like a kid having innocent, but destructive, fun. If a few tools disappeared, clothes got altered, walls got decorated, etcetera, his mom mildly scolded him and then defended his actions to Gus, saying his creativity got the best of him. He got mouthy with Gus, but it was never in his mom's presence. He learned to show nothing short of reverence for the man when she was around.

The result of all his conniving was that Gus truly despised the kid and his mom thought he walked on water. When Gus and Patty argued, it was almost always because of Avery. When Sunny came along, a demanding and colicky infant, their attention to Avery would waver and he would have to invent new ways to earn his mom's approval. He put up with Gus and Sunny, but his allegiance was to Patty and he never neglected to show her that.

When Avery turned eighteen the summer after graduation, Gus put his foot down and kicked him out. Gus said he had been forced to make his way at that age, and that Avery would be required to do the same.

Avery had blossomed after leaving that confounded household, taking a job at the local newspaper office, and enrolling in community college courses. Now twenty, he

10

had just gotten his associate's degree and was heading off to the University of Washington in the fall to study journalism.

Avery was telling his mom about the Omak mayor's latest stunt. The mayor had taken out an ad in the paper to find out whose Rottweiler was responsible for impregnating his Afghan Hound, with a reward, the pick of the litter, offered to whoever came forward. Sunny walked in as he was finishing his story.

"So the mayor said he knew the daddy was a Rottweiler because of the puppies' wide black snouts and their penchant for German sausage," Avery explained. His description of the brown and black mutts with their ridiculously long hair and desire for hot dogs had Patty nearly hooting with laughter.

Gus' annoyance had begun when Avery marched into their house without so much as knocking and then proceeded to grab one of *his* beers from the fridge. He continued to glower while Avery told his stupid story, and he reached his breaking point when he saw the look of complete adoration on Patty's pretty face. She thought he hung the moon!

"You better pay up for that beer, Avery," Gus started. "You have all this money for a fancy college education. You have your nose up in the air for getting to associate with the mayor. You're wearing a shirt with a goddamn pony on the pocket. Since when do you get to come into *my* house uninvited, take a beer like you own the place, and sit there telling stupid stories to your mother, who should have been cooking my dinner an hour ago?"

Sunny froze in the doorway, wondering how her mother would react to this attack on her golden boy.

"You're in a foul mood, old man. Mom, am I keeping you from making supper? I didn't come here to make trouble for you," Avery said.

"Actually, Avery, I have the steaks marinating in the fridge right now. Everything else is already made and chilling. It looks like I'll even have an extra steak for you since your asshole of a stepfather will be eating dinner elsewhere."

Patty had found some assertiveness in her new job. She had been working part-time with a road crew as a flagger. Thus, the word 'asshole' was becoming a regular part of her vocabulary as she faced down nasty drivers and stinky, cranky construction workers three days a week. As far as she was concerned, Gus was right in their league starting in on Avery.

Gus' face turned red and he flew into the kitchen. He was going to give it to Patty good for mouthing off about him. What he hadn't bargained for, however, was that his stepson, who was tired of his constant drinking and disrespect for his mother, had also gotten bigger over the last few years. He had been working out. Though he was still shy of Gus' six feet and two inches, he was well-muscled, strong, and, as always, much more passionate about his mother than Gus.

For the first time since he met Gus at five years of age, Avery took a swing at his stepfather. The blow, taking Gus by surprise, landed flush on his left eye socket. He stumbled backward, swearing. Sunny saw, as he pulled his hand away from his eye that Avery's knuckles had left her father's brow gashed and bleeding—a lot.

Sunny let out a short cry of alarm and as everybody turned and finally noticed her presence, she did what she always did at the sight of a fair amount of blood—she passed out and slid slowly down the door to the floor.

Chapter Three

There was a metallic taste in her mouth and a bright slant of light was trying to penetrate her loosely closed eyelids. Sunny came to as her mother held her brother's half-filled beer bottle to each of her cheeks in turn. The sun from the front window pierced her eyes so fiercely that she had to close them again. She must have bitten her tongue when her rear end hit the floor because she was certain the metallic taste was blood.

Blood. Oh yeah.

She remembered all at once what had been happening before the world turned black. Her normally implacable half-brother had socked her dad a good one. She hadn't seen that one coming. What she also didn't know was that her fainting had prevented further bloodshed. Because Gus had been very close to teaching his stepson a lesson in brawling, something he had acquired some skill at in his evenings at The Club. It was the sight of his scrawny, sun-burned daughter sliding unconscious to the floor with her blond ponytail trailing her that shifted his rage into alarm.

They may have had their share of fights recently, but she was his beautiful baby girl. Like him, she had Scandinavian features—strong bone structure, fair hair and skin, and, when she showed it, a brilliant, warm smile. She reminded him so much of his sister, Kaye.

Sunny would have loved her Aunt Kaye, who had been just as bullheaded and passionate as she was. Neither Kaye nor his fun-loving parents had lived long enough to meet Sunny—they had been killed at a train crossing on their way to watching him play high school football two towns away. Kaye would be forever fourteen in is mind, further emphasizing her similarities to the teenaged Sunny.

Sunny scowled at the offending beer bottle and then focused on her father's grave, bloody face. "Geez, Daddy, could you at least wipe some of that blood off? I really *don't* want to pass out again."

"Yep, she's okay. Already expressing her opinion," Avery immediately deadpanned.

Gus rose from his haunches, looked Avery square in the eye and told him without a word that he'd better get out now while his teeth were still intact.

"Mom, I'll see you next week at the Stampede Rodeo. Remember, I got us chute seats. Sunny, if you're not still feeling puny, I got enough for all three of us." Only Gus noticed the obvious omission of an invitation for himself. Not that he would want to go with Avery and his good-two-shoes pals. They would only annoy him with their holier-than-thou attitudes. They were just educated idiots, all of them.

"You be good, Avery. I'll call you next week to make plans," answered Patty. As he showed himself out, she walked the short distance to the guest bathroom and prepared a cool washcloth for Sunny's forehead. She welcomed the distraction of Sunny's condition. Lord knows what may have transpired if she hadn't shown up and stolen the show! Patty's first loyalty was to her son, but at least until Sunny was raised, she needed to keep peace with her husband as well. It was stupid of her to rile him up like she had done.

"You scared us, Sunny-girl," her father said.

"I always do that when someone's bleeding entirely too much. Remember when Crystal took that nosedive off the front of her bike? She was trying to avoid the Stevens' Great Dane and she headed straight off the edge of her driveway into her mom's rose hedge. The thing poked so many holes in her she had streaks of blood running down her arms and legs. That's how I ended up with so many scrapes of my own that day. One look at her and I was out cold, bike and all."

"Oh yes, I sure remember that day. Shawna Rinker called me and I raced over there. We weren't sure who to clean up first. You were just about as bloody as Crystal and full of driveway gravel. She had a ton of pesky thorns to pick out," Patty reminisced as she dabbed Sunny's forehead.

Talking about Crystal made Sunny's mind wander back to the earlier events of the day. She was trying hard to breathe with her mouth closed, because now her mother was right in her face, rubbing the washcloth across her brow. The smell of alcohol would be obvious if she were to let out a deep breath right now.

As for the other thing she had done, well, she didn't really feel any different, just a little sore and maybe a little sorry. She had pictured feeling more grown-up, like having sex would somehow make her wiser than she was before.

She mulled over what she would tell Crystal. She was, after all, her best friend and they had talked about who and when and what it would be like enough that she would have to tell her what she now knew—it wasn't at all like they thought it would be.

How on Earth was she going to tell Crystal what it was like without telling her who she had done it with? Duwayne was so much older than they were that Crystal had always been sort of grossed out by her childhood crush.

Besides, what if she told her parents? Shawna Rinker had been doing daycare long enough that she wouldn't put it past her to turn in her own son because Sunny was underage. She had heard of things like that.

Last year a senior girl at their high school had been busted when she slept with a sophomore boy after prom. Rumor had it that his parents had found them in the garden shed and, furious, had slapped the eighteen-year-old girl with rape charges. She'd lost a college scholarship and everything. Sunny didn't want anybody to make a big deal out of this.

She really couldn't tell her parents either. Lord knows she had been a difficult child, fighting fierce battles with both Gus and Patty, over even the smallest things. Ever since she could remember, she had needed more attention than they seemed to want to give. There had always been Avery to compete with—the obvious favorite. But as much attention as this news would garner, she didn't want to cause trouble for the Rinkers, something Gus would surely see to. They would probably never let her see Crystal.

She waited for her mother to rise, intent on retrieving Sunny a glass of water, and she popped up from the floor herself. Her head whirled once more and she shot out a hand toward the doorframe.

"Easy there, Sunny-girl," Gus said as he reached out to steady her. She still looked a bit green around the gills. He was going to at least see that she made it to the couch. As he reached around her waist, he caught a big whiff of her dry, alcohol-soaked breath.

His immediate reaction was that he was mistaken. Surely it was his own breath he was smelling. He and John Pierson had met at Upper Conconully Lake that morning. They had done some trout fishing and in the process had consumed a few beers.

Surely he was smelling the alcohol on his own breath. She was only thirteen for Christ's sake! To be sure, though, he took hold of her other elbow and pulled her toward him as if to embrace her. At the last second, he shifted his hands from her elbows to her cheeks and planted a kiss on her forehead. She let out a quick breath of surprise.

If Gus had been suspicious before, he was now completely convinced that his daughter had been drinking. To top it off, he was sure that what he was smelling was whiskey! His eyes widened in surprise and she knew that she was caught.

"Sunny Louise Moss! You've been drinking! And by the smell of it, it wasn't just a little taste, darlin'. You've got some serious talking to do. I want to know where. I want to know who with. I want to know how you got it. Goddamnit, Sunny, you better explain this minute."

"She's been doing *what*?" asked Patty from the kitchen doorway. "Tell me it's not true, Sunny."

"You bet I've been drinking. And I won't tell you who or how or what or any of that, Daddy. You two were the ones who chased me away in the first place because you never listen to me. Why should you care now what I've been up to? You don't deserve to know."

"We are your *parents*. You are only thirteen years old. What could have possessed you to try drinking?" Patty's voice was starting to take on a higher pitch, almost a whine.

"I wasn't *trying*, mother. I drank. I did it for fun. I did it to erase my parents who are so ugly to me. I hate you both for grilling me like this. It's summer. It wasn't a big deal. Besides, Daddy, you drink all of the time. Nobody asks you why."

"Sunny, I'm a grown-up. Don't you turn this conversation on me. Your mother and I do not approve of your behavior," replied Gus.

"I didn't ask for your approval. All I wanted was for you to *listen*. This is all your fault."

At the insinuation that she and Gus had some control over Sunny's latest stunt, Patty felt something inside of her snap. That thin, worn-out band of patience she had inside of her had finally had enough. All of the hurt and blame and ugliness came bubbling to the surface. She threw the glass of water she held into the sink where it shattered loudly.

Sunny's eyes widened and she prepared to bolt, as she always did when she knew she'd mouthed off past the limit.

Then Patty said something that Gus had never thought she would say to one of her children.

"Get out, Sunny," she said, now deadly calm.

"What do you mean, 'get out.' Where am I supposed to go? You are my mother. You can't tell me to leave. You have to take care of me," Sunny cried. She was confused. Something was going dreadfully wrong here.

"No. I can't do that any more, Sunny. I have taken care of you for thirteen years. I've shown you all of the love and patience that I can, Sunny. I've taken your insults, your pushes, your slaps, your abuse, little girl, and I have died a little each time that you didn't love me enough to stop. I've kept all of your viciousness wrapped up inside of me and I have always turned the other cheek.

"Now you're telling your father and I that it is our fault that you are stupid enough to be drinking at the age of thirteen. You're such a smart girl, Sunny—too smart to make these bad choices. You cannot lay this blame on us. I won't let you get away with it.

"I want you out of my sight. Go wherever it was that you got the booze and have some more, if you're so inclined. So help me, I have had enough of alcoholics in my life, between Avery's dad and Gus-- I'm done watching people self-destruct."

Gus moved to embrace his wife, "Come on Patty. You don't mean that. We just all need some time apart to cool off. Let Sunny go to her room and we'll fetch our own dinners and we'll talk about this reasonably later."

She shrugged him off. "Very well. Sunny go to your room. While you're in there, pack the things you'll need. I'll call Shawna Rinker and see if you can stay with them for a while. Lord knows you're there enough to be one of her children anyway.

"Gus, I see that you think I've flipped my lid, but I'm actually clearer than I've been in a while. We will not be raising this teenager. She has made it obvious that she prefers to grow up all on her own. I can help with that. Get moving, Sunny."

Sunny knew that her mother was telling her to move, but she couldn't get past her disbelief long enough to will her feet to go any direction. One thing was for sure. She felt stone cold sober now. She had always known that Gus and Patty didn't love her like normal parents did. They always had an agenda.

Shawna and Nirval, they loved their kids, gave them unchecked affection and endless freedom. Her parents were always nagging her to help with chores and do her homework and to wear less makeup and more clothes. They didn't understand her at all.

She'd never seen Patty so icy, so furious. She'd always turned and fled situations that got too heated with Sunny. That she was standing her ground now told Sunny that she meant what she was saying. So now what? She was going to live with Crystal? She wouldn't be allowed to stay in her own home? She'd have to take her things somewhere else? Then she thought with horror, 'I'm going to have to share a room with Crystal!'

She finally managed to get her body moving and eased past her father to head down the hallway to her bedroom. She felt a little like crying, but the shock of being kicked out had robbed her of her normal emotional responses. She first sat at the edge of her bed trying to think of what she should pack first. Then she realized that she had nothing decent to pack things in. Her old school bags were about all the luggage she had. So she set about stuffing them randomly and carelessly. The Rinkers were right down the road, after all, and after Patty cooled off, she would be able to come back. She was confident of this.

Gus had known his wife long enough to know when not to argue with her. He was also entirely battle-weary from his dealings with Sunny. He understood Patty's exasperation because he felt it himself. Perhaps the Rinkers really could do a better job parenting Sunny than they had. (Never mind that their nineteen-year-old loser of a son was still living at home.) Crystal seemed like a good girl. Maybe that was precisely the influence Sunny needed to keep on track.

When Sunny came back from her room with her five school bags filled with clothes and things, Gus took three of them from her and walked her to his green Chevy truck. He threw all of the bags in the back and opened the passenger door for Sunny. She climbed in and her Dad drove her the quarter mile to the Rinkers'. Patty had called and worked everything out with Shawna Rinker.

As her Daddy drove away, Sunny knew in her child's heart that she had lost two things precious that day. Home would never be the same and neither would she.

Chapter Four

The sweltering day was just heading into a gentle
summer evening when Sunny arrived at the Rinkers.
Shawna Rinker had the trailer doors open to let in the
evening breeze; and she was standing just inside the front
screen door, watching Sunny, as her shoulders slumped in
certain defeat. Her uncombed blond ponytail hung listlessly
down her back, looking as let down as she must feel. She
shifted her slight frame suddenly to kick a rock down the
dusty driveway, as if it had committed some offense by
being in front of her shoe.

Shawna's heart just about broke for the girl. She had
heard Sunny lay into her mom on more than one occasion,
and she'd always thought to herself, 'If that was my child,
I'd pop her a good one right on that smart mouth.' But
then Shawna, after three children and years of providing
childcare to other people, had never actually had to raise a
hand to any child. They had never disrespected her the way
that Sunny did Patty.

Shawna's amiable disposition appealed immediately to
children and she had a way of communicating with them
that required little more than a look or a gentle nudge or
a few well-chosen words. Children just naturally wanted
Shawna to like them and they loved to please her.

Most adults admired Shawna Rinker as well. She had big, round brown eyes that frequently glowed with mischief. Her honey-blond hair was perpetually pulled back into an easy ponytail which lengthened and shortened with regularity. She was petite, but strong and constantly active. Her home may have been in a colorful junkyard, but she kept a neat little lawn bordered by flowerbeds brimming with blooms. The inside of the 60's era mobile home was paneled and dark, but she kept it absolutely immaculate.

Shawna had raised three kids in that trailer with her husband Nirval. Their youngest son, Dawson Rinker, was enlisted in the Army and serving his time at Fort Bragg in Georgia. Duwayne was still at home—basically a good kid, but seriously lacking the ambition that his younger brother had. Because he shared Nirval's passion for American-made cars, he was working in the service area of the local Chevy dealership, where his dad was a manager.

Crystal had been sort of an afterthought. She arrived six years after her brothers and easily became the light of her mother's life. She'd had fun with her active boys up until then, but her little girl was her princess. She'd delighted in painting her room pink and surrounding her with dolls and pretty clothes. Much to her mother's chagrin, Crystal ended up being somewhat of a tomboy, preferring horseback riding to shopping and digging in dirt to playing with dolls. Despite this, the mother and daughter were great friends— they could talk about anything.

One of the discussions they had been carrying on lately had been about Sunny Moss. Shawna knew that Sunny had always needed more attention and approval than the average child. But the chip on her shoulder had grown into something too large for a thirteen-year-old to bear. She was starting to rebel. Shawna knew children well enough to recognize when one might be straying into deliberate misbehavior. Sunny was going to make some bad choices very soon. Shawna knew this in her bones.

She was also committed to making sure that Crystal, Sunny's best friend in the whole world, didn't go along with her. They had had frank talks about sex, drugs, alcohol, and getting good grades. Shawna had strong small-town values and she knew that, without Sunny's influence, Crystal would stick to these. But she was entirely unsure how much of a hold Sunny had on her daughter.

It was with reservation that Shawna had agreed to take Sunny in for a little while. She and Patty's friendship went back a long way. They had become acquainted when Shawna watched Avery and Sunny while Patty occasionally cleaned houses for extra spending money. The two found they had a lot in common since Avery and Duwayne and Sunny and Crystal were all the same age. They still met once a month for lunch to catch up with one another.

Shawna was well aware that Patty's patience with Sunny had been wearing thin. She had thought, but never voiced to Patty, that Sunny would have benefited from discipline at an earlier age. It was getting a little late in her life to start punishing her now. The damage was done. It was not surprising that Patty had completely lost control and that she now needed help with her child.

Even though she saw it coming, she still ached for Patty and Sunny, knowing that a rift had developed there that would probably never be healed. She and Crystal were lucky to have each other and she knew it.

In truth, she had accepted this responsibility for two reasons—she wanted to help Patty, but mainly, she could keep a closer eye on Sunny and Crystal's activities if they were both under her roof. And perhaps she might have a positive influence on Sunny in the meantime.

She exited through the screen door and walked up behind her new charge, slipped her arm around Sunny's slender shoulders, grabbed a few of her stuffed school bags, and led her inside.

Duwayne and Nirval were sprawled on the sofa watching TV. Duwayne completely ignored Sunny when she came in with his mom. Actually, he was playing it cool. He didn't want his mom to know the earlier events of the day any more than Sunny did.

Nirval sat up straight and said 'hi' to Sunny. He had always thought the girl had potential. He saw that she had a spark of intelligence behind her petulant guise. He got a kick out of teasing the girls when Crystal had Sunny over. He would tell them outrageous stories about the boogeyman and monsters in every crack and crevice. He'd made himself into a folk hero in their eyes--his version of Rinker and Okanogan County history made him bigger than life. They were all at once terrified and enthralled by him. Sunny had wished many times that Nirval Rinker had been her dad instead of Gus.

Crystal was in her room, cleaning up and transferring her clothes into the top two drawers of her dresser to make room for Sunny's things. She had always wanted a sister and was excited that her best friend would be allowed to stay with her. It would be super fun when school started and they could get ready together in the mornings, share clothes, ride the bus the whole way together, and share the day's gossip every night. She was thrilled that her mom was letting Sunny stay.

"Hi, Crystal," Sunny greeted her friend, sounding as sad and confused as she truly was.

Crystal had known Sunny since they were both in diapers. All it took was one look in her friend's eyes. She walked quickly to Sunny and took her in her arms. Sunny finally burst into tears and they stood together in that embrace while Crystal rocked her friend back and forth.

Shawna, her own eyes brimming with tears, stepped back into the narrow hallway and closed the door. She knew Sunny would be hungry once she was feeling better. She retreated to the kitchen to salvage her some leftovers.

It took a few days for Sunny to settle in. She was uncharacteristically quiet and Crystal thought it was probably because she was still so sad that she had been kicked out. They had gone a couple of times to Sunny's house when they knew her parents were at work to get some more of her things.

Crystal tried hard to make her tiny room work for the two of them. She knew that Sunny was used to her nice big room in their ranch house. She had a ton of stuff! A lot of it was going to have to be left behind if she stayed with the Rinkers in their small mobile home.

Sunny didn't really care about the stuff, though. Her

sullenness wasn't from leaving things behind. It was the result of having had the worst day of her short life and not being able to tell anybody the whole story. She knew how close Crystal and Shawna were and she just couldn't bring herself to tell Crystal what had happened with Duwayne. Nor could she tell her why Patty had gotten so angry with her because it involved alcohol that she had consumed from this house! All of the hurt and trauma and stupidity of that day were bottled up inside of Sunny and she really had nowhere to turn. She would have to confide in her friend sometime.

Sunny was by nature somewhat of a loner, but she had learned to trust and love Crystal over the years. There was no other friend who would understand her choices, no one else that she would even want to tell.

It was two weeks into her stay at the Rinkers when Sunny finally got up the courage to talk to Crystal about what had happened that first week of August. School was to start in few days, and Sunny's fourteenth birthday was coming up the week after that. They were discussing what her family would do about Sunny's birthday. Would they even acknowledge it? Patty and Gus had shown no signs of caring whether Sunny ever came home.

Crystal was increasingly curious as to what Sunny could have done to make them so unrelenting. "Are you ever going to tell me what happened?" she asked Sunny gently.

"I'm not sure I *can* tell you. I have wanted to ever since the first night I came over here, but I'm not sure what you'll think," replied Sunny.

"You know you can trust me. Have I ever told anybody

any of your secrets? And how many years have we been friends?" Crystal was contrite.

"You're right. But you can't tell anybody about this, Crystal. Not even your mom, 'cause she would never understand."

"Wow, this *is* serious! Come on. Tell me," Crystal implored.

"Promise me."

"I promise to keep it between us. Now spill." Crystal's curiosity was really piqued now.

"I had sex."

Crystal's mouth dropped open. "*With who?*"

Sunny sighed. She knew Crystal would have a million questions, so she decided to get it all out at once. "Okay, here's all of it: I had sex with Duwayne in the back seat of the rusted red Ford Fairlane at the end of the north row of cars. I was drunk on whiskey, which we swiped from your mom's stash under the kitchen sink. It wasn't his fault, Crystal. I let him do it."

Now Crystal knew why Duwayne had been so evasive. The guy was hardly home anymore, and he certainly avoided Crystal and Sunny when he was there.

She interrupted Sunny, "And you actually *told* your parents this whole story! *Why?*" She was incredulous.

"No. I didn't tell them any of it. They lost it when my dad smelled the alcohol on my breath. My mom said she'd had enough from alcoholics in her life. She basically hates me. My dad didn't do anything to stop her from kicking me out. I've always told you that they didn't care about me."

"Whoa. I'm still trying to get the whole 'I had sex'

thing. They don't even know about that?" asked Crystal, now confused.

"Nope. They flipped over the booze."

"Well that *was* kinda dumb, you know. We're only thirteen, Sunny. Drinking is a stupid choice. How many times has my mom told us that?"

"She's also given you and I lectures about avoiding sex until we're married. She's been telling us to 'just say no' to everything for so long I can't even remember when she started. Come on, Crystal. I was curious and I was mad at my mom and dad and it was hot and I was delirious. It was stupid. What else can I say?"

"You're right; it was stupid. And, ew. You had sex with my disgusting brother! Of all people you could have picked. I wish I had been home that day so I could have clocked some good sense into you!"

"Duwayne's not so bad. You know I've thought he was cute forever. He kind of talked me into it. I knew he'd be careful with me. And he's been a gem not to say anything to anybody. Some guys are too macho to keep that stuff to themselves."

"Yuck. That just makes me sick. Let's just forget that it was my icky brother for just a second. You have to tell me what it was *like*." Crystal's thirteen-year-old nosiness took over.

"Not that great, Crystal. All of the romantic fantasies we had about our first time, about how wonderful it would be and how good it might feel, they were wrong. It was quick and painful and I don't feel any different now. Just cheap. That's how it felt—cheap. I hope that you will be smart

30

enough to wait for someone special."

Crystal could tell that Sunny didn't want to talk anymore. And although she was mighty curious about the experience, she was truly sickened by the thought of her best friend with her much older brother. It was time to leave the subject alone.

"Okay, Sunny, let's go pop some popcorn and enjoy one of our last summer afternoons with a chick flick and air conditioning."

"Sounds good to me," Sunny sighed and smiled. At least she'd come clean to somebody. Now she could put her dumb stunt behind her and relax and enjoy the harmony that ruled the Rinker household. This could be a good year after all.

Crystal kept Sunny's revelation to herself for a whole week while they started school and planned her birthday party. Crystal was determined to make the day special for her best friend. Hopefully she could make her forget that her parents were yet to acknowledge that the day was approaching. If Sunny's family couldn't muster, then by golly, she could.

Shawna noticed that something was bothering her daughter right before school started. She could always tell when Crystal was keeping something from her, because she wouldn't meet Shawna's gaze. She would avoid conversations and cut her mother short when she tried to pry it out of her. It was ironic that the only times Crystal had ever behaved this way were when Sunny and she had secrets to keep. Shawna had never failed to get the truth from her daughter and she didn't plan to this time.

Shawna was as busy planning Sunny's birthday as Crystal was. In the Rinker household, a birthday meant favorite meals all day, birthday cake, and treasure hunts. The birthday person was made to feel special from the time he or she woke up until each went to bed.

Sunny's birthday was on a Thursday, so they would have to work around school, but she had learned that Sunny loved cinnamon rolls and ham and cheese omelets, so she would have both ready for her in the morning. She would also send a sack lunch to school with Sunny that had her favorite tuna salad sandwich in it and a note of encouragement. She was planning to make lasagna for dinner and top it off with a chocolate cake with chocolate frosting, Sunny's favorite food. Besides this terrific variety of foods she would prepare, she was planning an elaborate treasure hunt in the car yard.

Sunny had not been able to school shop with her own mom, so most of her clothes were from last year and were worn, faded, or outgrown. The Rinkers didn't have large means, but Shawna knew how to stretch a dollar. She frequently went to clearance sales at the end of each season at some of the fancier clothing stores. She would pick up things for Crystal or the boys in the size that she guessed they would be the next year during that season. This year she had underestimated how much Crystal would blossom during the summer. Her hips and rear were much too round for some of the jeans and her bust too large for some of the fall tops that she had picked up. Lucky for Shawna, Sunny was just a slip of a thing still, tall for her age, but with a body that was straight as a board. The clothes that hadn't fit

Crystal would fit Sunny perfectly.

She was going to hide three pairs of designer jeans and three matching tops in shiny packages throughout the yard to hunt for after dinner. That should complete a full, fun day.

Crystal was working on ways to make the school day more fun. She made a locker-shaped "Happy Birthday" poster to hang on Sunny's locker in the eighth-grade hallway. She made fliers that said, "Who's Sunny and Funny and Fourteen Today?" to hang on the bathroom doors. She even planned to do a "Happy Birthday" announcement over the PA system, since she was the student council PR person and she had access.

To top it all off, Crystal had bought Sunny the latest novel from her favorite author. After all, Sunny was the biggest bookworm Crystal had ever met. They had been talking so much lately, even until the wee hours, that Sunny had not had much time to read, but Crystal knew she would love the present.

All of the hoopla was sure to make Sunny feel the love she was trying to find at home. Crystal knew it would perk up her reticent friend at last.

It was Wednesday evening and all plans were in place at the Rinker household. Sunny had gotten a call from Patty, after all, recognizing her upcoming birthday. Sunny hadn't wanted to interrupt all of the activities the Rinkers had organized for her on her birthday, so she had gone for dinner with Avery and her parents that evening.

Shawna was glad to finally have Crystal to herself that evening. It was time that they talked about the big secret that Crystal was obviously keeping from her.

Crystal avoided her again, saying she had homework to do. Shawna promised her that she would help her with the homework if they could sit and talk for a few minutes. Crystal reluctantly agreed.

"You need to tell me what's bothering you, honey. You know we never keep things from each other. Just because you have a 'sister' now doesn't mean you don't need to talk to your mom, you know. Besides, I miss our talks."

"I miss talking to you too, Mom. It's just that Sunny told me some things and swore me to secrecy, told me that I couldn't even tell you. It's killing me, Mom, but I promised!"

"Crystal, I've taught you to honor your promises above all else and I admire that you've kept your secret this long. Is there anything that you can tell me that wouldn't hurt Sunny? Most of all, is there anything you can tell me that might keep Sunny from hurting herself?"

"She did some really dumb things, mom. I can't get specific, but Duwayne was involved. Remember when you told me that Sunny would start making some bad choices. Well, I think that time has come. I think as long as we keep her here and out of trouble, she'll be okay. She's already said she doesn't want me to make the same mistakes, so I know she won't pressure me to get into trouble."

"Well if Duwayne is involved, then I think I need to know what's going on, because both of those two are living here."

"No, Mom. Actually he's been really cool since Sunny came. He hasn't even looked twice in her direction. I don't think he'll do it again."

Shawna pounced, "Do *what* again?"

"Oh man, I said too much. Okay, I'm gonna spill, but you've got to promise to be cool about it."

"We'll see." Shawna held her breath and gazed steadily into her daughter's round, brown eyes, so like her own.

Crystal sighed deeply, "Sunny and Duwayne had sex. But it was a long time ago, Mom, before Sunny came to live here, and he doesn't seem interested in her now, and she won't do it again because she said it was terrible and I believe her." The words were rushing out now that she had begun to talk.

Shawna realized that she was still holding her breath. It left her like a blow to the stomach. This was so much worse than she had imagined! Her nineteen-year-old son had taken advantage of an underage girl! She had to know details. She had to know what she must do because she couldn't possibly turn back the clock.

"When did this happen and where, Crystal? What were they *thinking*?"

"Mom, I don't think they did much clear thinking. Did you notice that your bottle of whiskey had gotten sort of empty?"

"I thought maybe your dad drank it. So he got her *drunk* first? Oh God, Crystal. He could go to *jail* for this. Do you realize that?"

"Mom! I knew I shouldn't tell you. You're making a big deal out of this. He didn't take advantage of Sunny. She told me that. It was her choice, her curiosity. She knows it was a stupid thing for both of them to do."

"No, Crystal, I'm glad you told me. I needed to know what's going on beneath my own roof. If Sunny and Duwayne are carrying on, they will not be allowed to do it here. I obviously need to lock up the booze, too."

"But they're not still having sex, Mom. Sunny wouldn't want to do it again. It's done. You don't have to worry about it anymore."

"How do you *know* that, Crystal. Do you really think you can trust a girl who's doing the things you say she's doing to tell you the complete truth?"

"She's my best friend, Mom. We don't lie to each other any more than you and I do. It was hard enough for her to tell me the things that she did. I shouldn't have said anything to you!"

"It breaks my heart to do this, Crystal, but I'm going to have to ask Sunny to leave. As long as Duwayne is living here, which he will be doing for at least another year, I can't leave Sunny at risk like that. They've broken the law and they've violated my trust in them."

"No, Mom," Crystal begged tearfully, "She doesn't have anywhere to go. Make Duwayne leave, the loser. It's *his* fault. You can't do this to poor Sunny."

"*Poor Sunny* deceived me from the very beginning when she came to live here, knowing what she had done in my home," Shawna was unrelenting. She was sure Nirval would back her up on this.

"Be a good girl and start that homework. You will not change my mind on this. I have to talk to your dad and let him know what's going on."

Tears streaming down her face, Crystal merely hung her

head and did as she was told. She had committed treason against Sunny. Her mom would never change her mind. Her friendship was over and she knew it. Sunny would get kicked out once again. It was enough to break Crystal's heart.

Shawna was heartbroken too, but like any sensible mother, she was not to be blindsided again. After talking to Nirval, who was also devastated by the news, she called Patty to let her know that Sunny would have to find somewhere else to stay.

By this time, Sunny had returned from her birthday dinner. She immediately sensed that something was dreadfully wrong in the Rinker house. Like déjà vu she was being asked to pack her things again and get out. She did as she was asked in a daze. How did they know what had happened? Surely Crystal hadn't said anything?

Sunny was met with uncharacteristic coldness. Shawna Rinker informed her that she could stay the night, but that she would be required to leave the next day.

So Sunny Moss left once again to make her way on the first day of her fourteenth year. Shawna had at least given her some nice new clothes to take along. She waited for Gus' truck to arrive and she wondered where she would go next. Wherever it was, she knew that a piece of her soul was being left behind with the Rinkers, whom she loved wholeheartedly and whom she had betrayed unforgivably.

Chapter Five

Patty's arrangements were hastily made in light of the news about Sunny. Shawna Rinker had hated to add insult to injury by telling Patty the full extent of Sunny's transgressions, but she felt she owed her an explanation. Patty reacted first with shock and dismay, and then she reminded herself that she had already fundamentally failed in parenting Sunny. The revelation of Sunny's loss of innocence, while it saddened Patty, shouldn't have come as a great surprise.

After all, after thinking about it, Patty realized that she herself had made similar mistakes when she was only slightly older than Sunny. Her daughter was at a curious, rebellious age, and Sunny was doing what came naturally to her. The difference was that Patty had never blamed her parents for her own behavior and she accepted her own consequences, one of which had been birthing a child out of wedlock.

Sunny had been spoiled and, while she had missed her daughter during her recent absence, Patty was inwardly relieved that Sunny was no longer around to belittle and berate her at every turn. She was absolving herself of responsibility for Sunny's behavior because she had never had any control over her daughter. The price would be

Sunny's to pay.

Sunny would be going to live with her aunt, Gwendolyn Mota, in Brewster, the small south-County town that Patty had grown up in. Patty regretted that Sunny would have to change schools, but at least it was just the beginning of the school year. She knew that Sunny could not be allowed to return home. She and Gus were not doing any good parenting her. Perhaps a total change of environment would bring Sunny around.

Gwendolyn Mota was Patty's older sister. She was a forty-year-old widow who had not had any children. Her late husband, Alberto Mota, had died in his early sixties of heart failure. Alberto had been a successful orchardist, growing cherries and apples on a 200-acre orchard just a few miles north of the town of Brewster. He had started out as a migrant farm worker, never finishing any formal schooling. With sheer determination and living in abject poverty while he saved money for his land, he had built a small empire.

Because he had been so busy shaping his own American dream, he had not bothered to look for a wife until he was well into his forties. Gwendolyn had been the bookkeeper for the packing sheds he operated. She was smart and savvy, tall, shapely, and very blond. It was a source of pride for Alberto that she had shown any interest at all in an uneducated, humble Hispanic man like himself. He had wanted her to be his partner in every way, so they had married. Gwendolyn was twenty-five.

She had loved and admired Alberto. He had shown her great respect, allowing her unchecked freedom in running the business end of their orchard and packing sheds. He was in charge of what he loved and did best—cultivating and farming the land they owned.

For whatever reason, they had never conceived a child. It wasn't for lack of trying on Alberto's part and it caused him great distress that he had no sons to pass his legacy onto, especially when he started to have heart problems. Gwendolyn had been indifferent to the idea of being a mother. She was spread thin enough with work obligations and running their household. When Alberto became ill, she was somewhat relieved that she wasn't saddled with the additional responsibility of dealing with children.

So Alberto's legacy had been passed onto his young widow. Gwendolyn was now sole owner of Rancho Manzanillas. She ran the orchard and packing operations with cool precision, resulting in quality fruit and healthy profits.

The home that she and Alberto had built was like him— humble, but elegant. It sat in the middle of the orchard property at the peak of their highest rolling hill. The house was stucco with a red tile roof, a style that was common to the Southwest, but rarely seen in Eastern Washington, which dealt with harsh, snowy winters and extreme summer heat.

The interior continued with the Southwestern theme, with spare, but brightly colored furnishings, accented by blankets, baskets, and paintings by Native American artisans. Gwendolyn kept the bright, cheery three-bedroom home neat as a pin. She had just one companion, her cat Pericles, whose calico coloring made her blend with her colorful surroundings.

The main house gave way to a vast, sloping green lawn. Gwendolyn kept no flowerbeds because she had no spare time to tend them, but she had her orchard workers fertilize and mow the lawn frequently so that she had nice-looking surroundings when and if she entertained. Her only other concession to outdoor decorating was the terracotta urns that bordered her patio, filled to the brim with blooming, drought-tolerant annuals each spring.

Orchards planted in neat rows marched down the hillside in all directions from the residence. The orchard gave way on the north side to two large packing sheds—one devoted exclusively to cherry packing and the other equipped for peaches, pears, and their biggest crop, apples. Parking lots surrounded the sheds. The south side of the orchard was flanked by migrant worker housing, which consisted of twelve tiny, white cabins with green trim and a larger cook/community cabin in the center.

Gwendolyn managed all of this with keen intelligence and a firm belief that she needed to know *everything* that went on at Rancho Manzanillas. She handled the financial details and relied on her foremen to inform her of all other details in day-to-day operations. She frequently dropped in at the shed and at the migrant community house to monitor the goings-on. She was fair and friendly to all who worked for her, but she tolerated absolutely no mischief or misconduct. She was greatly respected and feared, and she liked it that way.

It was with trepidation that Gwendolyn offered to house her wayward niece. She'd always thought that she had no business raising children. After all, she had no time for them. She did have space, though, in her home for Sunny and it sounded as though Patty was at the end of her rope with her daughter.

Gwendolyn really hadn't gotten to know Sunny during these fourteen years. She got yearly school pictures from Patty and dutifully updated them in the frame on her bureau. Patty's family also had her over each Christmas Eve, along with their mother, Margaret. The yearly gathering was obligatory and conversation was often stilted and tense.

She and Patty and Margaret's history was ugly and complicated. The sisters had little love, but a suffocating sense of responsibility to their mother. Margaret had been single since their father had left them when Gwendolyn was five and Patty was one. She had worked as a waitress to support them, often doubling shifts just to get by. Margaret was always, in a word, tired. She had resented her two daughters simply for existing and making life such an enormous effort. She hurled verbal abuse on a regular basis; and until they were too big to shove around, she did a little of that too.

It seemed to Margaret that it took forever, but when her daughters were finally raised, she washed her hands of them. Gwendolyn got a job right away and moved into her own place, not expecting her mother to work to support her any longer. And she sent money regularly to her mother to help with Patty's teenage expenses. Patty had gotten pregnant right before she graduated from high school and Margaret had done the only logical thing—she kicked Patty out and told her to go live with the worthless young man who got her into trouble in the first place.

But Patty's worthless young man had wanted nothing to do with her or a baby and had denied all responsibility, so Patty went to live with her now established older sister. The young women had agreed that their mother was awful and that they were glad to be free of her; however, they did owe her a certain amount of respect for raising them all on her own.

Patty got a job clerking at a local convenience store and they did their best until she had her baby. Gwendolyn became Avery's back-up mommy during his very early years until Alberto Mota came along. Then Patty moved to Okanogan. Gwendolyn still loved Avery dearly, but she knew how much work and struggle had gone into having that baby in her household.

Sunny was no longer a baby and Patty once again desperately needed her help. Of these facts, Gwendolyn was sure: Margaret could never be allowed the burden of another child to support. Patty couldn't turn to friends in the Omak or Okanogan area because Sunny's antics were well known to their acquaintances. Patty couldn't live with turning her daughter's care over to the State. Living with Gwendolyn would be her last resort.

Gus had the job of delivering Sunny from the Rinkers to Brewster on her fourteenth birthday. He still had not found the guts to stand up to Patty and let Sunny come home. He basically liked Gwendolyn and thought that perhaps Patty was right to teach Sunny this lesson. Gus knew that he hadn't been helpful in trying to raise Sunny. After all, he was rarely around. He was at work or at the Club. He hadn't the courage to change that pattern to take on his difficult daughter. He did know, though, that he would like to kill that Rinker boy for bringing about all of this trouble.

Sunny was sullen throughout the ride. She didn't like to cry in front of her dad. He never knew what to do or say when she did that. So she tried not to think about Shawna and Crystal and their disappointment in her. She tried not to think about the hard mask that was now her mother's face every time Patty looked at her, tuning her out, erasing the emotion from their relationship. She tried not to think about the fact that she was going to live with someone that she hardly knew and be forced to go to school with strangers. Any time she thought about that, tears would start to well up behind her eyes.

Instead, Sunny looked out the window and focused on the passing landscape. She admired the perfect farms and neatly planted orchards and car-laden homesteads that were separated by miles of sagebrush. She stared out at the winding Okanogan River approaching and departing the vicinity of the highway as they traveled South. Her new home would be very near the mouth of the Okanogan as it dumped into the Columbia River. About halfway to Brewster she counted the cars on the freight train that coursed along the track parallel to the river.

Gus and she didn't speak. He didn't try to give her a pep talk. What could he say? It's not like he could do anything to change her situation. This was just a break for all of them. She'd come home eventually, when she straightened up her act. '*If* she straightened up her act,' he thought.

By the time they reached Rancho Manzanillas, Sunny had pushed all of the sad thoughts from her mind and resolved to make the best of her new surroundings. She had always known that her parents didn't love her, but at least they had found her a place to live again. Her attitude had gotten her into trouble in the first place, and she was going to check it at the door. Aunt Gwendolyn would get her very best behavior.

As they climbed the hill leading to the main house, Sunny marveled at the endless rows of apple trees bursting with the ripe fruit of the season. The orchard buzzed with activity at the impending harvest. It seemed everywhere she looked were apple bins stacked to the sky, ready to receive the bountiful fruit.

All of the people she saw were compact, athletic-looking, and colored some shade of brown. She would learn later that all of Gwendolyn's migrant farm workers were originally from Mexico or Guatemala and that many of them returned every year to Rancho Manzanillas to work for the Motas.

They pulled into the circular drive at the front entrance of the main house. Gwendolyn stood on the front steps, tall and regal against the door jam, with her arms crossed over her chest. Her face registered a calm that she didn't feel and she forced herself to be still as Sunny emerged from her dad's truck.

Sunny had always admired her aunt's blond sophistication and her no-nonsense demeanor, but she trembled a little when she saw Gwendolyn's serious visage.

Would Gwendolyn be nice to her? Or was she in for a rough life in this beautiful place? She took a deep breath for courage and walked up the steps, bags in hand.

"Hi, Aunt Gwendolyn," she started and gave her a winning smile.

Gwendolyn, taken aback by Sunny's warm greeting, couldn't help but smile back.

"Hi, Sunny. Since we're going to be seeing a lot of each other, why don't you call me Gwen. It's much easier."

"Okay. Gwen," Sunny replied.

Gwendolyn nodded at Gus as he dropped the rest of Sunny's bags on the second step, "Hello, Gus."

"Hi there, Gwendolyn. Say, we appreciate you taking Sunny for a while....."

"Don't mention it, Gus. Tell Patty 'hi' for me." And with that she dismissed Sunny's father. She had never had any use for Gus. Besides, she needed Sunny to herself now so that they could figure each other out. She was as new to this as Sunny was.

"Okay, Sunny-girl, you take care now." And with that, Gus hopped back in his truck without looking further at his daughter and, Sunny noted, without the hug that any kid with normal parents would expect.

She shrugged off the last thought and turned back to Gwendolyn.

"Show me the ropes, Aunt Gwen. I may be here a while."

Gwendolyn, seeing the slump that had overtaken Sunny's shoulders, took Sunny's hand and said with a wink, "Won't that be great fun for us girls?"

Chapter Six

Gwendolyn showed Sunny her room. It was at the front of the house, where the early morning sun would greet her each day. Gwendolyn had picked this room because it was Pericles' favorite bed in the house. She surmised that made it comfortable at least.

Sunny instantly loved the red, yellow, and green wool Pendleton blanket that covered the bed and the rough-cut, lightly-stained log furniture throughout the room. Pine bookcases flanked the window seat at the opposite side of the room, inviting her to sit and read, something she enjoyed doing. Because she had never had a lot of friends, books had taken their place for as long as she could remember. She'd missed reading at the Rinkers'.

Pericles opened an eye when they entered and stretched herself as she mewed a quick greeting to her mistress.

"You have a cat!" Sunny exclaimed in delight. "She's so cute!" She sat on the edge of the bed and, to Pericles' delight, started stroking her orange and black mottled coat.

Gwendolyn warmed to her favorite animal and her niece starting off so nicely. This just might work out.

"Her name is Pericles. Looks like she likes you, Sunny.

"I should warn you that I'm not normally here much during harvest. I took the day off to get you settled in. This is the busiest time of year here at Rancho Manzanillas. I want you to understand that you may be on your own a lot."

"As crowded as it was at Rinkers, I think I might enjoy time to myself," Sunny replied, continuing to pet the cat. "Besides, Pericles can keep me company."

So far this girl was not at all what Gwendolyn had expected. Patty had led her to expect someone sullen or surly. Sunny seemed determined to be positive about her circumstances.

"Did Mom tell you that it's my birthday? This is such a wonderful room. I think getting to stay here is a perfect birthday present, Aunt Gwen."

Oh, no. Patty had not mentioned Sunny's birthday and Gwendolyn hadn't even noted the date. What a horrible day to have to go through so many changes! She decided to be honest.

"No, Sunny, Patty didn't mention that it's your birthday. I'm glad you like your new room, though. How about we go to lunch in Brewster to celebrate? I can show you around the town a little."

Sunny brightened at Gwendolyn's suggestion.

"Okay, Aunt Gwen. I would like to see where I'll be going to school on Monday. And I'd like to know where the library is. Can we have Mexican food for lunch?"

"I know a great place," Gwen replied.

Sunny started school the following Monday. She dressed in her new clothes, combed and curled her straight blond hair carefully, and put on tinted lip gloss (the only makeup Aunt Gwen thought she needed.) She looked fresh and sweet, two things she had never wanted to be, nor claimed to be, in her old school. Her former ways of dressing and acting tough were behind her. These kids didn't know her, so she could be who she wanted to be. She wanted people to think that she was happy and well-balanced and came from a good family. She didn't feel the need to be popular—that had never appealed to her—but she didn't want to be known as a complete rebel either, which she had been at home.

She signed up for art and library research as her electives. All of her teachers seemed competent enough. They introduced her in each of her classes, which embarrassed her, but she just smiled and waved to her classmates each time and endured any questions that they had.

She and Gwendolyn had agreed that she would take the bus to and from Rancho Manzanillas because Gwendolyn would be too busy to pick Sunny up. But on Wednesday evenings, Gwendolyn had a series of meetings for local growers that she needed to attend. She decided to let Sunny stay in town those afternoons so that they could meet for dinner and Sunny could spend some time at the local library.

Sunny had discovered right away that the North Central Regional Library system was an excellent source of information. Not only was just about every book you could think of available, but it offered an expansive list of periodicals, magazines and newspapers that Sunny enjoyed reading just to keep up with current events.

The Brewster library was small and quiet and Sunny

got to spend untold hours on Wednesdays just pouring over information on everything from politics to art to teen issues. She read novels at Gwendolyn's house, but her time at the library was spent satisfying her growing curiosity about the world.

She was also becoming particularly interested in painting. She had taken art classes in the sixth and seventh grade at Okanogan, but they had been mainly about art history, drawing, and sculpting. She had never taken a class that focused on modern art and painting. As it turned out, her art teacher had called her a natural at blending colors and shapes. Mr. Bruins had even told her that she might be a budding abstract artist. Nobody had ever singled out a talent of hers in such a way. He encouraged her to keep practicing, which she did before school and during lunch hours.

Sunny, who had always been a loner, and who had so recently been feeling abandoned by her parents, was starting to blossom with a renewed sense of peace and hope. Gwendolyn expected her to complete basic household chores—laundry, dishes, and weekly dusting and vacuuming—but she recognized that Sunny was a kid and gave her plenty of free time and autonomy. Besides, Gwendolyn was so busy that Sunny was often left to her own devices, to fetch her own dinner and complete her homework by herself.

Gwendolyn was delighted with her niece's progress. She reported weekly to Patty how well Sunny was behaving and what a pleasant housemate she had become. Patty and Gus were pleased to hear that someone had finally gotten through to Sunny. To Patty this meant that she had made the right decision and that Sunny was better off in Brewster. To Gus, this meant that they had been too hasty, hadn't given Sunny enough of a chance to shine, and that they should give her another opportunity to come home. The Moss' spent bitter hours arguing over whether Sunny should return to them. For them, peace was far out of reach. Perhaps it had always been.

Sunny spent the winter and early spring cultivating her newfound talents for art and research. This left little time for meeting the new people that she went to school with. But there was a Hispanic girl that she repeatedly ran into in the art room before school and at lunch. She learned from Mr. Bruins that the girl's name was Yolanda and that she was two years ahead of Sunny, making her a sophomore in high school.

Yolanda was also a talented artist, but her interests ran darker. Her paintings often featured bleeding bodies or tortured faces or, as Sunny later learned, gang symbolism and violence. The images were haunting to Sunny and because Yolanda seemed as much of a loner as she herself was, she decided that she had to get to know the girl.

Sunny knew how sacred it was to give an artist her time to work and she didn't like to interrupt her own practice time in the art room, so she waited until a Wednesday after school to approach Yolanda on their way out of the school building.

"Yolanda? Hi. I've seen you around, but you don't know me. I'm Sunny Moss. I like your paintings."

Yolanda spoke with a thick accent. Sunny would learn later that she was Honduran.

"Hello, Sunny Moss. I am Yolanda Juarez. I like your paintings too. They are very colorful. I can't make sense of them, but they are pleasing to me."

"You're probably not interested, because I'm just an eight-grader, but I'd like to talk to you sometime about your pictures. I don't see very many people spend as much time in the art room as I do."

"I knew you were only in the eighth grade. I asked Señor Bruins about you. That does not mean that we can't be friends, does it?" Yolanda replied.

"I asked him about you too! He must think that we are real losers for not just talking to each other!"

Sunny and Yolanda laughed. Sunny told Yolanda that she was on her way to the library and Yolanda walked with her because it was on her way to her house. They found that they had a lot in common. Yolanda lived with her grandmother because her parents had sent her from L.A. to get away from the gangs she'd been involved with there. Her grandmother was busy raising the other five grandchildren that she had been saddled with and so Yolanda also got a lot of time to herself.

Sunny told Yolanda that she lived with her aunt, but she didn't tell her why her parents had sent her away. She would save her little gems for until she knew her new friend better. They talked about other things—their paintings, their brothers, and some of the other kids they went to school with. Both enjoyed the other's company. A friendship was born that early spring day in the crisp air beneath the newly awakened foliage. Neither knew that the friendship would carry them far from this place and these circumstances. They just knew that it felt good to be together.

If either Yolanda's grandmother or Sunny's aunt had known what mischief would befall this alliance, it would have never flourished, but who can know these things? Sunny and Yolanda sure didn't.

Chapter Seven

Sunny's contentment lasted until late spring when Gwendolyn decided to rock the boat.

"Have you decided where you're going to work this summer?" Gwendolyn began.

"What do you mean? I've got plans for the summer, but they didn't include working."

"What sort of plans?"

"I've got a list from Mrs. Evans of summer reading. I wanted to get a good start on it for next year."

"You could do that after work hours," Gwendolyn reasoned.

"But that's not the only thing! I also wanted to practice painting outside. Mr. Bruins had some good ideas for me to work on during my free time."

"Couldn't you do that too? After work?"

"There won't be any time! Why do I need to work? I know Mom and Dad send you money for my food and clothes. Why should you be able to dictate the use of my free time? Who do you think you are?"

So this was the spirit that had Patty tied in knots. Gwendolyn could see Sunny's temper flaring. What Sunny didn't plan for was Gwendolyn's calm demeanor and her gentle appeal to reason.

"Well I certainly don't think I'm your mother, for one thing. Don't get all excited about this, Sunny. I didn't realize that you had a practical agenda for the summer. All I'm trying to say is that you could accomplish all of that and still learn responsibility and the value of the dollar."

"I just don't see how that's possible. What would I do with the money anyway?"

"Haven't you gone by the window of Paulson's Department Store and wished that you could buy that pair of designer jeans? You know the pair I'm talking about—the jeans with the sparkly thread through them."

"You know that I have, but Mom would never buy them for me. So she would say they were too expensive."

"When you're earning your own money, you get to decide what's too expensive and what you would really like to have. Am I getting through here?"

Sunny was exasperated. As much as she wanted to argue with Aunt Gwen, she couldn't deny the truth of what she was saying.

"I don't like to issue ultimatums, Sunny, but I really believe that having a job would be good for you. If you want to stay here, you'd best think about complying."

"You don't have to say it, Aunt Gwen. I get it. Find a job this summer or else, right?"

"Did it sound that awful?"

She nodded and smiled at Gwendolyn's obvious discomfort, but she got the message. Sunny excused herself to her bedroom so she could think.

Sunny desperately wanted to stay at Rancho Manzanillas. She liked the life she had built here in

Brewster. She grudgingly agreed to take a job hand-thinning apples. It would mean horridly early mornings, as early as four a.m., but she would be done by noon and if she could still move, she could spend the rest of the day doing the things she wanted to do, painting and reading. Besides, thinning would be done by mid-July and she would have a whole month before school started. It wouldn't be so bad really. She would finally have some money of her own to spend.

Even better, Yolanda needed a job as well and had agreed to thin apples with her. Yolanda wanted to buy a car at the end of the summer, so she was going to spend mornings thinning with Sunny and afternoons cleaning houses with her grandmother.

Gwendolyn used chemical thinning on most of the orchard, but hand-thinning still had to be performed to assure the apples' shape and color, so she hired a large crew of thinners, thirty including Sunny and Yolanda. The foreman was Pedro Lopez, a man that Gwendolyn had trusted for many years. He and his wife lived just a half-mile from Rancho Manzanillas and they were considered a close part of the orchard family. Gwendolyn knew she could expect Sunny to be a master thinner with Pedro as her mentor.

The day after school got out for the summer, Sunny dragged herself out of bed at four a.m. and pulled on shorts and a thin, long-sleeved cotton shirt. Her arms needed the protection of the sleeves, but the heat of late morning required breathable cloth. She brushed her fine hair back into a pony tail and brushed her teeth. For breakfast, she grabbed an apple to munch on her way down the hill.

Pedro had the crew gather at the northern base of the orchard, where the older trees grew. They would start at the bottom and work their way counterclockwise around and then up the hill.

All of the thinners were first-timers, so Pedro set about showing them which of the fruit needed to be removed and how many should be taken off. He showed them how to most effectively pop the small apple from the tree. Sunny would learn from Pedro that she could use gloves for this job, but that she would be much faster and more effective using her bare hands. The job paid by the hour, but thinners were relegated to other jobs very quickly if they could not keep pace with the rest of the crew.

Most of all, they were warned that very large old trees that they were working on required ladders to reach the tops. They were to be mindful of the ladders at all times for their own safety. Pedro and five of the other thinners, also strong young men, would be in charge of moving the ladders as needed.

Sunny noticed the first morning that Yolanda was acting strangely. Both girls fell easily into the rhythm of thinning, a job which left no time for visiting. During their break, Sunny noticed that Yolanda seemed particularly watchful of one of the young men on the crew. The guy was about eighteen, good-looking, Hispanic, and all muscles and very white teeth, so it was understandable that Yolanda might be interested. But Sunny already knew her well enough to know that Yolanda wasn't being flirtatious. She seemed to be nervous.

She waited until their first day was completed to approach Yolanda and see what was up.

"Hey, girl. Are you as sore as I am? I feel like my fingers could never grip another thing again! I noticed you looking at that guy, Miguel, kind of weird-like. Do you know him or something?"

"You know, Sunny, I am not sure if I know him or not. I may have to call some old friends in L.A. I just hope he is not who I think he is. Listen, I have to hurry down to the shed. My grandmother is picking me up there so that we can go clean two houses this afternoon. I'll talk to you later."

Yolanda was in such a hurry to go each day that they didn't get to talk to each other until the end of the second week. By then Sunny was in a dither over her friend's complete avoidance of Miguel. Sunny had talked to him a few times and he seemed very friendly and harmless. He liked to talk to the 'blonde senorita,' as they had nicknamed Sunny.

"It's Friday, Yolanda. Do you have to rush off again today? Or can I finally visit with my friend for once?" Sunny asked.

"I am sorry, Sunny! You know how much I want a car. My grandmother gets a lot of jobs because she is such a good cleaner. She had to take today off to take my cousins to the clinic. Did you want to hang out?"

"Yeah. Let's go up to the main house. Gwendolyn won't get home until late tonight, and I can fix us a decent lunch while we catch up."

Sunny had never asked Gwendolyn if she could have somebody over, because she and Yolanda had not had that kind of a friendship. They had always met at a neutral place, not at each other's houses. It was sort of an unspoken understanding that the places they lived were entire worlds apart, that their class and culture would forever be a fissure between them.

Sunny was bridging that gap little by little by working in the orchard with Yolanda and now by asking her to her house. Yolanda, recognizing this, but still feeling uncomfortable going to the 'boss lady's' house, chose another meeting place.

"How about if we meet at the lunch room in the cherry packing shed? I will buy you lunch since I am making *big* money now," she teased.

"No way. You have to save for that car. My money is only for stupid things like clothes. I'm buying lunch today," Sunny countered. She wouldn't press the issue of having Yolanda over to the main house, but she wouldn't let her spend her car money either.

They arrived at the cherry shed at twelve-thirty. Most of the shed workers took their lunch break at eleven since they were off at three-thirty, so the cafeteria was almost empty. Gwendolyn kept a kitchen crew year-round so that any of her workers could have a hot, healthy meal in the middle of the day. It was something Alberto had insisted on, along with the gym and indoor basketball court at the apple shed. He had always wanted his employees to live happy and fit, figuring this would improve longevity and decrease turnover. He was right—their employees were fiercely loyal and most were in great shape.

Sunny and Yolanda ordered turkey subs and cups of corn chowder. They sat at a small table near the door. Sunny noticed that Yolanda again seemed nervous, glancing around repeatedly and talking softer than she was accustomed to hearing.

"When are you going to tell me about Miguel?" Sunny finally asked about halfway into lunch.

"What about him? He seems nice enough, does he not?"

"You're avoiding the question! Why? You told me you were going to call L.A. and you're acting all nervous and stuff. Something's not right about him, is it? You act like he has the plague.

"You don't want him to notice you, do you? That's kind of hard to do, you know, when you're totally gorgeous and totally skinny with great big brown eyes," Sunny teased.

"You are too sweet, Sunny, but I am afraid that Miguel has already noticed me. That is why I avoid him. I was not sure at first, but now I know that he is the little brother of a boyfriend that I had in L.A. He looks so much like Julio. That is why I asked my old friend about him."

"Well, that's good, right? This old boyfriend doesn't hate you or anything, does he? Is that why you're so scared?"

"Sunny, we have always been able to talk about the things that we have in common. But we have never talked about your past, like why you live with your aunt instead of your parents. I have not asked because I did not want to share my past with you.

"I am going to tell you now, though, because I can tell that you are worried about me. Sometimes I feel fifty years old with all I have seen. Are you sure you want to hear this?"

Sunny nodded solemnly. Yolanda continued.

"We left Honduras when I was ten. We were very poor and it took us a very long time to steal into California. We worked our way slowly up the coast of South and Central America and through Mexico. My mother, my older sister, and I, we all sold our bodies to earn money to make our way here. My father and my younger brother panhandled. My brother would act like he was blind and sing songs all day in town squares for money. My father kept an arm bound to his side to look like he was a cripple. At the end of the day, we would return to whatever shelter we had built on the fringes of whichever town and endure our family dinner in silence.

"All was sacrificed—innocence, pride, everything—so that we could become Americans. My father truly believed that we would have a better life here and perhaps we have. But the things we had to endure are unspeakable and I will not tell you any more about that.

"When we reached California, my uncle, who had been in America for ten years, got my father a job in a convenience store in L.A.. My mother and my sister, who was sixteen, worked as maids at a small motel. My eight-year-old brother and I got to go to school. We had a tiny little apartment, but life got better.

"By the time my sister was nineteen and I was fourteen, she had landed a rich boyfriend. He had a hot red corvette, a thick gold chain with a cross around his neck, and several gold teeth to match. He made it clear that he had money and he showered my sister with gifts. His name was Rafael Suarez. He was smooth, let me tell you.

"When his younger brother, Julio showed interest in me, I jumped at the chance to date him. What I did not understand was that both brothers were involved with a gang that made and sold Meth, with ingredients smuggled from Mexico. They were getting rich selling drugs to kids. And, to tell the truth, we wouldn't have cared what they did except that one night while my sister was out with Rafael, on their way to a movie, a rival gang went after them. They shot both of them and left the scene. Both of them died before they reached the hospital.

"Julio and I were devastated, but also very angry. I went along on several trips that involved payback for what the other gang had done. Not everybody who was hurt or killed deserved it. I know that now, but it was all done in the name of revenge.

"My parents eventually heard about my activities from neighborhood friends. They still grieved the loss of my sister and they were afraid that the same thing would happen to me. So they sent me to Washington to live with my grandmother two years ago."

Sunny took all of this in, amazed at her friend's obvious resilience, and sickened by the waste of it all. She and Yolanda just looked at each other for a while as Sunny absorbed the story.

"Yolanda, I am so sorry that all of that has happened to you. It really explains why you paint like you do, but, I still don't get it. Why would it be a bad thing for Miguel to see you? I would think that you would be old friends and that you would be glad to see him."

"In a way, I was really happy to see Miguel. It brought back good memories, as well as bad. Julio was my first love. He was flashy and bold and exciting. He looked out for me. I was his girl. But I have kept in touch with old friends in L.A. and Julio was angry when I left. For one thing, I knew exactly what sorts of activities he had been involved in. I could get him in a lot of trouble. For another, he had loved me too, and my parents would not tell him where they sent me. They knew that trouble would come to me if Julio ever found me again.

"The best I can hope for now is that Miguel is not in touch with his family. Maybe he escaped all of the gang stuff. Maybe that is why he left California. I hoped at first that he would not recognize me, but I know that he has. Now I am just trying to work up the courage to talk to him. I am afraid of the answers he will give me."

Sunny pondered. This was quite a story and there was little she could do about Yolanda's past. She decided that the best she could do was be there for her friend should she get into another bad situation.

"I understand now. It doesn't matter, though. We'll just keep working hard, Yolanda, and it'll all work itself out. Miguel really is a nice guy. I don't think he wants trouble either."

"The problem is, Sunny, that trouble wants me. I have never been able to avoid it. I just have a terrible feeling that my peaceful life in Brewster is about to change, and not for the better."

The next month was uneventful at Rancho Manzanillas. The thinning crew progressed uphill through the orchard and Sunny progressed through her summer reading list. Gwendolyn realized that her niece was a rather talented artist as she began to fill the walls of each room with simple canvases that complemented each room's colors and mood.

Gwendolyn encouraged Sunny's newfound talent by buying her a new set of paintbrushes and a briefcase-sized case of acrylic paints. She called it an early birthday present. Sunny had borrowed an easel from Mr. Bruin for the summer. She set herself up with a makeshift studio on the sun porch and she often painted when the afternoon sunlight was the brightest, making her bold splashes of color all the more cheerful.

She had tried to put Yolanda's revelations out of her head. She hoped that by not thinking about the things they talked about that she could forget they ever happened, like she had done with her own mistakes. Now that she had Yolanda's young life to compare to, she realized how foolish and small-minded she had been. Her mistakes were petty compared to the life-changing events that her friend had been made to endure. It made her feel lucky to have had life so good so far. If she ever got up the courage to talk to her parents, she would be sure to tell them that.

She hadn't wanted to call them, despite Gwendolyn's encouragement to do so. Her superstitious mind told her that talking about her happiness would jinx it for her. She wasn't about to take any chances. She knew that Patty got weekly reports from Gwendolyn about her good behavior. Gus would know she was doing all right, too. Besides, if she got them on the phone, all she would do is blubber. She missed them terribly and Avery too, despite herself.

She still hadn't told Yolanda her reasons for living at Rancho Manzanillas. In fact they hadn't talked much at all. Yolanda still avoided Miguel and any conversation they had during work hours was stunted by Yolanda's fear of saying anything that he might overhear.

With just two weeks left in the six week thinning season, Yolanda's worst fears came true. It was a Friday, and she and Sunny had decided to do something fun together. They had been working way too hard and Gwendolyn had promised them a ride to town to catch a pizza lunch and an early movie. They were walking down the main road to meet Gwendolyn at the apple shed when trouble arrived.

It came in the form of a chili pepper red Chevy Blazer. They could hear the thump of music from fifty yards away as the tinted windows shielded the driver and passengers from their immediate view. Miguel, who had been walking several yards in front of them toward his own car, let out a whoop and with that killer smile spread across his face, ran toward the vehicle. Sunny and Yolanda stopped to see who was driving this mysterious car. The blackened window lowered as Miguel approached.

Sunny looked over to Yolanda just as her browned skin turned pasty and her eyes became wild with panic. Miguel looked their direction and gestured toward them. Yolanda, without a moment's hesitation, dropped her bag and took off running toward a stand of huge, old Red Delicious trees. Sunny could only gawk as her friend ran away and the driver of the car exited and booked after her.

Perhaps he wouldn't have looked so ominous if Sunny hadn't noticed the pearl handled pistol he had neatly strapped into a shoulder holster. The whole moment wouldn't have been nearly so scary if the man hadn't had complete rage written across his face.

Her only coherent thought as she watched Yolanda run for her life was, "This must be Julio."

Chapter Eight

It didn't take long at all for Julio to catch up to tiny Yolanda. Miguel and Sunny simply watched as he tackled her and they both rolled into the nearest trunk. Scared as she must have been, Yolanda didn't scream or put up a fight as Julio pinned her down.

Sunny finally found her legs when the two of them came to a stop. She tried to go help her friend when Miguel grabbed her elbow and held her in place.

"Let me go. I have to help her. He'll kill her, Miguel."

"No, Sunny, he won't. He is my brother. I know. It is okay, blonde senorita. He loves Yolanda. Watch."

Having no choice, Sunny did watch. Julio and Yolanda didn't speak, but just stared at each other, catching their collective breath. Sunny marveled as their expressions changed from rage to fear to hesitation and then, miraculously, Julio smiled and Sunny breathed a sigh of relief as Yolanda smiled back. Yolanda had been right. Miguel and his brother did bear a striking resemblance.

Sunny reddened and turned to talk to Miguel as Julio and Yolanda started kissing their welcome. Judging by Miguel's obvious discomfort, he didn't want to watch them get reacquainted either. They walked back toward Julio's Blazer.

"I promised my aunt Gwendolyn that we'd meet her at twelve-thirty and she's so busy that I don't want to be late. Can you just tell Yolanda, when she comes up for air," she rolled her eyes and smiled, "that I went ahead without her? It looks like she might be busy for a while."

"Okay, Sunny. I will tell her. I will see you Monday."

But Sunny didn't see Miguel Monday or for the rest of the two weeks of thinning either. She could tell that Pedro was annoyed that his thinning crew had been reduced by two—Yolanda hadn't shown up either. The rest of the thinners had to scramble to get the job finished in time.

Gwendolyn heard that Sunny's friend had been a no-show, and she also knew that Yolanda hadn't come with Sunny on the fun day they'd carefully planned for Friday. When she questioned her, Sunny told Gwendolyn about Yolanda's Friday visitor, but she couldn't tell her anything beyond that because she didn't know anything.

Sunny was a little worried about her friend, but mostly she was annoyed. She was having to work an hour longer in blistering heat every day to make up for her friend's absence and Yolanda hadn't even so much as called to tell her if she was all right or why Julio was in Brewster. And since she was stuck at the orchard for pretty much the rest of the summer, Sunny resolved to forget about Yolanda and her troubles for the time being. There was little she could do even if Yolanda was in some kind of danger.

Sunny had gotten so used to her early morning work routine that when thinning ended, she decided to take a job in the cherry packing shed, working just a half-day, still painting and reading in the afternoons. She was learning more and more about hard work and the satisfaction of doing a good job.

She had also learned how respected and admired her Aunt Gwen was at Rancho Manzanillas. She only hoped that someday she could be as smart and beautiful and accomplished as her aunt. She wondered why her own mother was so different from Gwendolyn. Sunny had never met Alberto Mota, but she knew Gwendolyn would never have married a man who drank like Gus nor settled for the life that Patty seemed content with.

One thing was for sure. Sunny would never settle for a boring little life at home with no education and bratty kids and a drunk husband. She knew that life had so much more potential than that and she was determined that she would have it. It took getting kicked out a few times, but she was figuring it out.

She even thought that maybe it wasn't such a good idea having a friend like Yolanda. A girl who left a job without notice and hung out with drug dealers; a girl who, at sixteen, was as worldly as any middle-aged woman; that kind of girl could only bring her trouble, couldn't she? She should look for a nice friend—a friend like Crystal had been, for instance. She should look for a friend that she could actually invite home for sleepovers and movies.

It was all very logical, as far as Sunny was concerned. That Yolanda was a kindred spirit with a tortured soul like her own was something she knew only subconsciously. Perhaps that is why, despite all her attempts to forget about Yolanda, she still missed her friend desperately.

Mid-August marked the demise of Sunny's easy life in Brewster. Margaret Smith, Sunny's fair-weather grandmother, was forced to move into the main house at Rancho Manzanillas. The circumstances surrounding her arrival made her presence all the more unfortunate.

As soon as her girls had left home, Margaret had married the owner of the café she'd worked at for years. Howard Smith had made innuendos for as long as she could remember, but she had ignored him, knowing first of all that he was very married and second of all that an affair would be no good with her two kids in the way. She did have standards, duly set after her loser of a husband had left her and the girls high and dry.

Howard's wife died two years before her youngest daughter, Patty, unmarried and pregnant, had left home. Margaret had seen no reason to keep Howard at bay any longer. Their children were grown and Howard was already a daily fixture in her life. Besides, she would do well to marry a business owner. He was a respected member of the community. His health wasn't the greatest, so he was low risk—if it wasn't working out between them, she could always wait it out until he knocked off.

As it turned out, she and Howard were great companions. The mutual respect that they had working together carried over into their marriage. Margaret was devastated when he died just ten years later. He had been working the grill because the cook had called in sick and he just keeled over dead right in front of her eyes, greasy spatula in hand. It hadn't been such a bad way to go, but she hadn't been ready to lose him.

Margaret sold the business because she simply didn't have the heart to work the restaurant any longer without Howard. She stayed in their house on Bridge Street and spent the next ten years avoiding the hard work it seemed she had done all of her life.

Instead of taking another job, she took on a few hobbies. There was not an acquaintance or family member in the greater Okanogan County that didn't have a knit doily or scarf from Margaret Smith. Sewing had been a chore when she had been forced to make clothes for her girls to save money. Now she took a shine to making quilts and fabric clocks with her old sewing machine. Game shows and talk shows became the background noise of her industriousness.

When she wasn't shopping for craft items or popping into her daughters' busy lives, Margaret became somewhat of a hermit. The sitting required for each of her hobbies took its toll on her once svelte figure. Her constantly benched bottom became decidedly round and her middle soon matched. Food was necessary, but fixing it took far too much time out of her creativity, so she opted for quick-fix, processed foods.

Margaret was disgustingly happy with life—until the money ran out. Howard had built quite a nest egg and she had been sure that it would last her the rest of her good years. But it couldn't hold up to her spending habits and inability to budget. Notice first came in the form of overdraft statements from the bank. She called them, sure that there was some sort of mistake. Indeed there wasn't.

Her liquid assets were gone. Basically all she had left was the house and its contents (and a veritable treasure trove of quilts, clocks, and knit scarves.)

This revelation came in June of the year of Sunny's arrival at Rancho Manzanillas. Margaret was sixty, and it would be several years before her social security would kick in. Out of desperation, and unbeknownst to her daughters, she began a weekly rummage sale that would last that entire summer. Slowly the contents of her life and home began to disappear. Gwendolyn found out about the liquidation when she happened to drive by her mother's yard on Bridge Street and noticed her grandmother's brass bed among the valuables being displayed on the small lawn.

Margaret pooh-poohed away her eldest daughter's concerns, saying that she just needed to clean out the house a bit and that she never liked that heavy old bed anyway. Gwendolyn, though, feigned thirst and invited herself in to Margaret's house. When she walked through an empty living room and into a kitchen with just four glasses in the cupboard and a hole where the dishwasher used to be, her curiosity turned to dismay.

It took only one look at Gwendolyn's obvious alarm to reduce her overweight, destitute mother to tears. She confessed everything immediately and Gwendolyn took it all in calmly, bought the brass bed for far more than it was worth, and headed home to contemplate it all.

The next day, Gwendolyn returned to Bridge Street and assessed Margaret's finances. She used her business knowledge to set up a strict budget for Margaret to follow and saw to it that she got signed up for food stamps and state-funded health care. She would have to sell the house because utilities and upkeep would eat up what she had left. Gwendolyn called a friend and got Margaret a low-rent apartment in a local, government-subsidized apartment complex. Even with all of this help, her mother would still be out of money in a little over a year.

Sadly, Margaret had become so sedentary that getting a waitressing job would be an impossibility and there was nothing else that she'd ever done or knew how to do. She could certainly never take care of children, Gwendolyn thought wryly. It looked like, ironically, her children were going to have to take care of her.

As it turned out, it was almost exactly a year later when Margaret ran out of money. Thus, she arrived at Rancho Manzanillas with just a few clothes, her precious sewing machine, and a bag full of knitting supplies and yarn. Accompanying her was a voracious appetite and a meanness born of poverty. Margaret's life had been reduced to almost nothing and she was damned mad about it.

She immediately took offense to the fact that Sunny had the nicest, biggest bedroom aside from the master and that it was closest to the living room and kitchen. Margaret felt Sunny should have given up her room to accommodate her aging grandmother. Gwendolyn wouldn't hear of it. Sunny had settled in so nicely and had made the space her own so thoroughly that Gwendolyn didn't think it would be fair to move her out.

Margaret had a perfectly comfortable, north-facing bedroom awaiting her. True, it was on the opposite side of the house from the kitchen, but Gwendolyn secretly thought it would do Margaret good to have to walk a ways to food. She wasn't doing herself any good by limiting her activity level.

Sunny's goodwill gesture to Margaret was to paint her an abstract that matched the camel, cream, and burgundy corduroy patchwork quilt on her brass bed. Margaret's reaction when she heard the painting was Sunny's was to blanch and tell her it looked like road kill on a hot road. She demanded that it be removed as soon as possible. She also told Gwendolyn to trade the quilt for another that was cotton—corduroy would chafe her and be much too hot.

Margaret also required shades that could black out the room. Curtains were simply too sheer to cover the daylight that the hilltop house provided. Also, the grandfather clock in the hall outside her room ticked much too loudly. It would have to be moved or find a different home altogether.

She complained about Sunny's early hours at the shed and that, despite the fact that Sunny's room was clear at the front of the house, her early departure was waking Margaret up much too early. She didn't like Sunny to paint while she was up and about because the fumes were extremely nauseating to her.

She accused Sunny of being standoffish because she spent so much time with her nose in a book. She went as far as insinuating that Gwendolyn was a lesbian because she worked so hard and managed the orchard like a man would. Her logic was that Gwendolyn would have had children if she had 'normal' tendencies.

Gwendolyn could escape Margaret's incessant

ugliness by going to work, but Sunny's world was turning increasingly black again as she endured day after day with her unhappy grandmother. She couldn't wait for school to start so she could escape. She'd see to it that she got to spend more time at the library and in the art room after school. Then she'd only have to see her grandmother from dinnertime on and she thought she could probably handle that.

All she knew right now was that she couldn't take this much longer. Something had to give soon.

Chapter Nine

School started the last week of August. Gwendolyn took Sunny to Spokane for a weekend to shop for school clothes with her hard-earned summer money. They took in two movies and shopped each day until they were both exhausted and fell into bed each night.

It was the most fun Sunny had ever had preparing for school. She got the clothes and supplies that she needed, but mostly she got the attention from her aunt that she had always craved from her mom and dad. Why hadn't her parents ever done this with her? Was it the money or the effort that was lacking? She couldn't help but wonder. Perhaps Margaret was right and Aunt Gwen was just spoiling her. All she knew was that she wished the weekend would last forever.

To Margaret, the weekend did last forever. Sunny and Gwendolyn had been helping prepare her meals and do her laundry. Without them, she had to do everything for herself. What really ticked her off was that Gwendolyn left only healthy food, things that she would have to chop, steam, grill, or fry to eat. Gwendolyn detested processed foods and she wasn't about to let her mother get away with eating them all of the time.

Margaret5 was in a foul mood when Sunny and

Gwendolyn swept through the door Sunday evening carrying bags and boxes full of Sunny's new treasures. They were all smiles, which soured her all the more.

"Don't suppose you left anything in the stores, did you Sunny?" she asked as soon as the two of them finished unloading the car and Gwendolyn went off to unpack her own bags.

Sunny had been starting to unload her bags when she noticed Margaret's tone. Her head snapped up and she directed her gaze toward her grandmother. What she saw in Margaret's eyes was resentment, plain and simple, and she began to armor herself for what was sure to be a battle. She started the conversation on a positive note.

"Hi, Grandma. Nope. I didn't leave anything behind if I could help it! We had a wonderful time. Did you enjoy your time to yourself?"

"You're a spoiled little girl, you know that Sunny? Don't pretend like you're not. Just look at all that stuff. Who needs that many clothes to go to school? Only spoiled little brats do, that's who."

Sunny didn't know what to say. She didn't want to make things worse, but she did want to stand up to her grandmother. She was getting pretty tired of being walked on.

"I used my own money, Grandma, that I earned all summer. Aunt Gwen said that I deserved to treat myself. She also said that my list of things I wanted was appropriate. It sounds like maybe you didn't have a good time while we were gone and I'm sorry for that."

"Yeah, you're sorry all right…," her voice trailed off as

Gwendolyn came back toward them from the master suite.

Margaret had begun to tread very carefully when Gwendolyn was involved because she wanted to be in her daughter's good graces at all times. Her livelihood depended on it. Gwendolyn had made it very clear at the end of her first week there that Margaret would make an effort to get along with both of them, or else. Margaret didn't want to know what 'else' was.

For some inexplicable reason, Gwendolyn was awfully attached to Patty's scrawny, stray daughter. She supposed that it stemmed from childhood. Gwendolyn had always been the child who adopted and protected just about any stray animal she could find.

Only Margaret truly knew the trouble Sunny had caused Patty. As far as she was concerned, the girl would never be reformed. She was simply smart, pushing the right buttons with Gwendolyn and making her way just as Margaret was. Well, if it came down to it, Margaret was going to prevail in the battle for Gwendolyn's affection.

Sunny had no idea that she was embarking on such a competition. Perhaps that was why she was so confused by her grandmother's hostility. 'Why does she hate me?' she would ask herself repeatedly. Margaret had never been cruel to her when she lived at home. In fact, she had made Sunny things, including her favorite Raggedy Ann wall clock, which still hung in her bedroom at home. She had never thought ill of her grandma, until lately.

As Gwendolyn came down the hall, she tried to smooth things over, "Grandma thinks we may have bought out the stores, Aunt Gwen." She smiled winningly, giving no hint that she and Margaret had been about to bicker.

"Well, we just about did, didn't we Sunny. We shopped 'till we dropped, Mom! It was so much fun."

"It *was* fun, wasn't it? We'll have to make it a yearly tradition, okay, Aunt Gwen?"

"Now I know why all my women friends want daughters. They make great shopping partners. Sunny kept me abreast of all the new trends and she kept me shopping when I might have quit if I was all by myself."

"Well, dears, that's nice that you had a good time," Margaret offered. "I'm going to turn in. I'm just exhausted. You two sure know how to make an old decrepit woman fend for herself!"

Gwen rolled her eyes when her mother's back was turned and then gave Sunny a conspiratory wink.

Margaret retreated to her room to watch television and stew over her continuing misfortune.

Sunny started school the next week. She soon settled into her old routine of hanging out in the art room and at the library. Unfortunately, though, her home life was nothing like last year. Margaret was making her miserable. Every time Gwendolyn's back was turned, Margaret was at Sunny, telling her what a brat she was, that she was sucking Gwendolyn dry. A normal teenager would be allowed to live at home with her parents, instead she had been turned out to an aunt in a whole separate town.

Trouble was, Sunny was starting to believe her. She had been doing so much better here in Brewster, but yet her parents had made no move to ask her to come home. Why was that? Was she that unlovable?

Even her brother, Avery, had made no effort to at least visit her when he was home from Seattle. Gwendolyn told her that he was planning to go to law school at the University of Puget Sound the next year. She was proud of him, but she never got the chance to see him to tell him that.

It was all so confounding to her, so she just continued to try and do her best. But despite her efforts, her attitude was starting to veer toward apathy yet again.

She hadn't made any new friends and school was pathetically boring without Yolanda. She still didn't know what had happened to her friend, but she did hear through people who knew that Yolanda had dropped out and was with her old boyfriend, Julio. Rumor had it that they were doing things they shouldn't be, drugs being at the top of the list. From the sound of it, Julio had himself a hefty drug dealing business. No wonder he had such a nice car.

If rumors were flying about Yolanda and Julio's activities at school, you could bet that the police were also catching on. Sunny wouldn't judge her friend yet, though. It was all speculation anyway, but she was plenty worried about Yolanda. If only she could figure out how to contact her.

Brewster was a small town, but people who were avoiding the authorities and rival gangs could make themselves disappear pretty easily into the backroads, orchards, or mountains in the area. All you really had to do is have a house with a nice basement, relatively big lot, and no snoopy neighbors and a drug dealer could thrive

·unchecked for years.

Without Yolanda around, art class had little of its old flavor. Sunny was missing the intensity of Yolanda's art. The rest of the class was doing bubble-gum and soda pop kind of work, while she was trying to elicit portraits and depictions of real life people and situations. Her worsening attitude about life was translating into pictures of darkened, lonely junkyards and abandoned animals and frightened children. Mr. Bruins sensed the mood change in her painting and as impressed as he was with the progress she had made over the summer, he was concerned with the direction her thoughts were leading her.

Sunny's birthday came and went with a special dinner at Camperos and a birthday cake, but with minimal ado. The fall turned into a winter as gloomy as Sunny's young heart. She moped home each evening, sure she couldn't take any more of Margaret's torture. As it turned out, she wouldn't have to.

Night came early during the winter in Washington State, so when Sunny arrived home from school at four-thirty on a November evening, daylight was already waning. She entered the house quietly, knowing that her Aunt Gwen was still working and trying to avoid another confrontation with Margaret.

She was hungry, so she tiptoed to the kitchen and grabbed an apple and a piece of cheese and took them down the three stairs to the sunken living room. Turning on lights would clue her grandmother in that she was home early on a night that she normally went to the library. Margaret would want her to fix them both dinner and most likely she would want to pick a fight. So, to avoid all of that, she settled into the deep, cozy couch. Pericles snuggled next to her as she set about eating her snack as silently as possible.

"Who's here? Sunny is that you, girl?" She heard her grandmother shouting from her bedroom doorway.

Unwilling to disrupt her quiet, comfortable moment, Sunny ignored her.

"I know someone is here. I can hear you. I may be old, you stupid girl, but I am not senile. Don't try to hide from me, Sunny, or I'll beat you silly with this cane when I find you. You've got chores to do, dinner to fix. You're not going to get away with this."

Sunny could hear Margaret shuffling her heavy body down the hallway and she wasn't sure why she wasn't turning on lights along the way, but with all of her grandmother's shouting and the continued darkness, all she could do was freeze and wait for what came next.

"You selfish, spoiled brat, I'm going to find you lounging around and I'm going to kick your worthless behind."

Sunny heard her own bedroom door slam open. Pericles let out a low, terrified mew, but Sunny stayed still.

There was almost no light left to the day, but she could still see her grandmother's ample silhouette outlined in the living room doorway. Sunny wasn't sure if Margaret could see her, but she remained still.

Then her grandmother did the inexplicable, and with no light to guide her, started down the stairs. Sunny could only watch with horror as Margaret stumbled on the second stair. Her huge torso twisted at a grotesque angle from her legs. Sunny heard an ominous snap and her grandmother's agonizing scream as she fell in a heap to the living room floor.

Still frozen, Sunny could hear Margaret moaning softly. Sunny was completely horrified at what had happened just because she wanted a little peace and quiet. Margaret had been right this whole time. She *was* a selfish, spoiled brat. A million thoughts were racing through her brain.

It was several moments before Sunny was able to move. Pericles had stayed next to her the whole time, so she now shoved her off her lap and scrambled to the phone. Margaret was apparently unconscious because her moaning had stopped, but she was still breathing raggedly.

She dialed 911 and told the operator what had happened and where to find them. Then she scrambled around her grandma's twisted body and ran to her room to grab a small bag of clothes, a brush and toothbrush, and her paints and paintbrushes. She scribbled a quick note to Gwendolyn to let her know how sorry she was about what had happened and to tell her not to worry. She would make do.

She ran out of the back door of the house and into the orchard just as the ambulance lights were approaching the bottom of the hill of Rancho Manzanillas. She was going to really miss this place. It had been 'home' more than any other place she had lived in her life. But she was leaving. She had to. She just couldn't face her Aunt Gwen when she found out that Sunny had caused Margaret's grave injury.

How could Gwendolyn ever forgive her when she would never, ever forgive herself?

Chapter Ten

The temperature dropped to twenty degrees overnight. Sunny wasn't prepared to stay outside in such weather, so she hid out in an empty picker's cabin for the night. It was still unheated and she had to put on almost all of the clothes she had brought with her just to stay warm. At least it hadn't snowed. She was totally unprepared for that.

She would have to find another place to stay. Her first thought was that she needed to get home to Okanogan, but then she thought better of that since her mom wouldn't be any happier with her than Gwendolyn was. That ruled out, she didn't have a whole lot of options.

One thing she did know. Yolanda would help her—if she could find her.

She set out just before dawn and followed the path of the highway to town, staying just out of sight of the road. For all she knew, someone might be looking for her. She secretly hoped they were.

Sunny arrived at Yolanda's grandmother's house just as her cousins were headed to school. She sidled up beside the oldest, Cassandra, about a block away from the house.

"Sunny! You scared me! What are you doing here?" Twelve-year-old Cassandra asked.

"I don't have a lot of time to explain. I'm in some

trouble and I need to find Yolanda. She's the only one who can help me."

"Yolanda's in pretty deep herself. Are you sure you want to do that?"

"I'm sure, Cassandra. She's the only friend I've got. Please tell me that you know where she is."

"Yeah, sure, Sunny, I know where she is. She's holed up with that no-good drug dealer, Julio. My grandmother is just sick about it. She was trying to keep Yolanda from trouble."

"I don't want to see Yolanda in trouble either. Maybe I can help her. Where does Julio live?"

"He lives on the Bridgeport Bar."

Sunny sighed. The Bar was a fabulous place to hide, with homes and Game Department land fanned out for miles along the Columbia River as it snaked toward Bridgeport and Chief Joseph Dam from Brewster. There were at least a hundred homes, all with acres of land around them and plenty of places to hide. She was going to have some hiking to do.

"All you have to do is get to the Game Preserve and follow the dirt road to the end. Take a left into that driveway and follow it to the end. The house looks like a shack. It's the shop behind it where you will find Yolanda and Julio and Miguel and all that they have been up to.

"The trick," Cassandra continued, "is that they don't want to be found. My younger sister and I have gone out there once, because Yolanda asked us to bring some of her things, but they were expecting us, and the guys still had guns tucked into their pants. They may not like you sneaking up on them."

"I'll take my chances. I need Yolanda's help and I need a place to stay. Thanks for your help. Wish me luck."

"I'll do more than that, Sunny. I'll pray for you, and my cousin too. I don't know what all she's mixed up in, but none of it is good. Don't tell Julio that I told you where to go. Goodbye, Sunny."

'Such a grown-up little girl,' Sunny thought as she walked away, forgetting that Cassandra was just three years younger than herself. She wondered if anyone in Yolanda's family ever got to just be a kid. Maybe the younger ones, she hoped.

Shaking off these thoughts, Sunny set off on foot, determined to walk as far as she could while it was still daytime. She didn't dare hitchhike in case someone was looking for her

As it turned out, Sunny didn't need to hitchhike. She felt and heard the bass before she saw the car it came from. The music was like rap, but the words were definitely not in English. Curious, Sunny swung around just in time to see a chili-pepper red Blazer headed her direction.

The vehicle slowed as the tinted driver's side window lowered. Miguel flashed her a brilliant white smile, as he waved a quick greeting. He turned down the stereo.

"Hey, there is that beautiful, blonde senorita I've been talking about," he gestured to her for the benefit of his passenger.

Sunny smiled and looked past Miguel to see who he was talking to. His passenger was Caucasian, like herself, but he had a thick shock of red hair, sticking straight up, and a slim mustache and goatee that matched. He had wiry, muscular arms, covered in tattoos all the same blue-green color. He nodded a greeting solemnly at Sunny and she got her first glimpse of very green, very intense eyes.

She thought he looked like the devil himself.

She broke her gaze and turned her attention back to Miguel.

"Hi Miguel. Listen, I've got some trouble and I need to find Yolanda. Can you tell me where she is? Isn't that Julio's car?"

"You talk too fast, Sunny! You gonna have to slow down poquito! You want to know about Yolanda and the car, sí?"

"Sorry, Miguel. Yes."

"Yolanda is with us. Julio and Raymond and me, we have a house on the Bar. You wanna see?"

She nodded.

"Get in."

She hopped in the back of the Blazer and Miguel cranked his deafening music back up as they drove the several miles back to their place.

Julio was not happy to see Sunny. He scowled at Miguel and Raymond as they told him about their visitor. The last thing he needed was some white girl poking her nose into their business. Would his little brother ever learn that it was best for them to keep to themselves? With his loud music and flashy ways, he was for sure going to attract the wrong kind of attention.

Besides that, Yolanda didn't need a friend around. He

couldn't stand it when girls got together and gossiped, tittering and giggling all of the time. His mother and sisters had done that and it had driven him 'loco.'

Yolanda was his. He had come all the way from California to get her back. He didn't need any of her old girlfriends interfering.

Sunny sensed his resentment the minute she was introduced to the infamous Julio. She just wanted to see her friend, not make Yolanda's life difficult. She was immediately submissive.

"It's nice to meet you, Julio. I can see you don't want me here, but I don't plan to cause any trouble for you. I didn't have anywhere else to go and I was hoping Yolanda could help me."

Julio reluctantly told Sunny that she could find Yolanda in the house. He gestured that direction, expecting her to find her own way.

It gave Sunny her first chance to really look around. The house was, as Cassandra had said, just a shack, small, with faded, graying wooden siding. It had a decided lean in the Northerly direction. It truly looked as if a stiff wind could have blown it down.

Stacked along the house were several worn-out propane cylinders and a huge flat of antifreeze. Bottles of nail polish remover, small cans of drain cleaner, and shiny silver cans of paint thinner lay scattered about the dirt yard looking like they'd been tossed randomly from the scraggly birch trees bordering the property.

The crowning glory of this dump was the shop out back. It was huge, white with red roofing and trim and blackened windows. Two green dumpsters, their tops propped open by overflowing garbage, blocked her view of the side door.

Sunny couldn't believe that Yolanda and all three of the men lived together in the tiny house. As she approached it, she saw Yolanda smile and wave through the grimy kitchen window, which had been taped with duct tape. She waved back enthusiastically.

Yolanda came running out the front door and embraced Sunny.

"Sunny! I am so glad to see you. I have missed you! I have not had a girl to talk to in a while. Not since my cousins came to visit."

Sunny gave her a quick hug and stood back to look at her. Something was off. The quiet beauty that Yolanda normally radiated had disappeared. She was still pretty, but she was rail-thin. She looked unkempt—her raven hair was dull and unbrushed and she had smeared too much black makeup around her dark, dull eyes.

It wasn't necessarily just her looks that were off. Yolanda's eyes darted about, and she shifted from foot to foot as if it bothered her to be still. She seemed almost to be humming, giving off a weird kind of energy. Her subtle dignity had transformed into uncertainty. What on earth had gotten into her?

"How *are* you, Yolanda? I've missed you too."

"Well, I am staying busy, cooking and cleaning for these silly men. I really don't go anywhere, because I have so much to do here. It is not so bad, though. I forgot how much I loved Julio. He is my man, Sunny, sexy and commanding. And he says he loves me too…."

She continued, saying more in ten minutes than Sunny had ever heard her say. She couldn't tell if Yolanda just missed company so much that she couldn't stop talking, or if she was nervous, or what. It was just unsettling.

Sunny finally interrupted, "Yolanda, I need your help. I didn't know where else to go. That's why I'm here."

"What happened? Are you okay?"

"I am, but a lot has happened since we last saw each other. My grandmother, Margaret, came to live with Aunt Gwen and me. She was awful, terrible to live with. To make a long story short, Yolanda, I think I may have killed her."

"You *what*?" Julio wasn't going to like this. Sunny might be bringing trouble with her. Trouble was something he liked to avoid.

"Well, she's hurt real bad anyway. She fell down some stairs while she was looking for me and I heard a pop and she was passed out and I just ran, Yolanda. I can't stand blood, so I didn't even try to check her out. I just knew that Aunt Gwen would be furious with me, so I grabbed some of my stuff and I took off."

"Did you at least call for help?"

"Oh. Of course I did. I just left before they got there."

"Okay. Well it sounds like it was an accident. Nobody could get arrested for that. Have you tried to call your aunt?"

"No. Yolanda, it was totally my fault. I didn't answer when Grandma called me and I left all the lights off. I knew it was dangerous, but I didn't call out to her. If she's well enough to talk, Grandma will for sure blame all of this on me. And who is Gwen going to believe—her own mother or her trouble-making niece?"

"Okay," Yolanda was still shifting around uncomfortably, "I need to think. I cannot think, Sunny. Maybe we just need to go inside. You can help me finish making lunch for the guys. We can talk more. We do not have a lot of room, but you are always welcome here."

Sunny followed Yolanda inside with growing apprehension. She could see that Yolanda had tried to make the shack homey. It was at least neat inside, but her worst fears about what was happening to her friend were confirmed as soon as they entered the kitchen. Yolanda had laid out bread on paper plates for sandwiches and set out mayonnaise and cheese and lettuce.

But Sunny's eyes were drawn to the edge of the sink where a glass pipe lay perched, as if it was ready to be washed with the rest of the dishes. It was blackened from the smoke it had contained. She swung around and saw more of the devices and a fresh packet of IV syringes on the kitchen table.

Sunny tried to play it cool. What did she think she would find with all of the rumors she had heard? This totally explained Yolanda's behavior and appearance. She was using. That punk Julio was drugging her best friend. This was new territory even for Sunny. She had always been the troubled one among her friends, but she had never done drugs. How was she going to help Yolanda? She had come here for help herself.

Yolanda was too keyed up to notice Sunny's trepidation. She immediately went to work on the sandwiches, yanking open the fridge to grab bologna and beers to go beside each plate at the table. She quickly cleared away the paraphernalia and piled it all on the counter next to the first pipe. All of this was accomplished in minutes, Yolanda chattering the whole time about 'Julio this' and 'Julio that.'

She finished and looked up, almost startled to see that Sunny was still there. "Let's call the guys."

"Yolanda, it's not even ten o'clock in the morning. Are you sure they'll be ready for lunch?"

"Is that all it is? Wow. I did not know that it was that early. These short days get me confused sometimes. But we will tell them it is a snack, yes?"

"Okay, Yolanda. Let's go get them." Sunny headed for the door.

"NO, wait, Sunny!"

Sunny drew back quickly, unsure what the trouble was.

Yolanda smiled nervously. "You cannot go out to get them. They are in the shop. We must never go in the shop. I went in one time when I first came and Julio came unglued. That is a private place for them. I meant that we should call them, yelling from the door. Then they will come in."

She went to the stoop and hollered, "Julio, Miguel, Raymond. I have made a snack for you if you are hungry."

The reply came back, sounding as if it came from a cave, and in Spanish.

"Miguel said they just had breakfast only a few hours ago. They are not hungry," Yolanda translated. Then she suddenly burst into tears.

Alarmed, Sunny grabbed a paper towel and started to dab at Yolanda's tears.

"I do not know what is wrong with me, Sunny. I cannot

seem to get things right. I cook constantly and clean the house, but it seems like it is never done enough or at the right time. Now all of this good food is going to go to waste. Julio will be angry."

"No way. We're going to cover all of this up with plastic wrap or paper towels and put it in the fridge for lunch. It will be just as good by then.

"Julio doesn't get mean with you when you mess up, does he? I mean, does he hit you?"

"No, no, Sunny. He would never hit me. He calls me his goddess. He just has rules, but he is the most perfect lover. We get high together, Sunny, and it is all very erotic."

"Stop. I don't want to know. Why are you using drugs, Yolanda? Did you do that in California, too? I'm not being a prude. I'm just worried about you."

"Don't worry about me. The crystal just helps me get more done. It gives me more energy and it makes my times with Julio more exciting. And it is making my body better, too. Did you notice how thin I am now? Nice, no?" Yolanda did a little spin, holding her arms out at her sides to emphasize her twig-like figure.

"No. You are too skinny, girl. I thought you were gorgeous with curves. All I want to know is this: Are you happy? Because that is all that matters."

"I am deliriously happy. I have everything that I want and need. I would be happier, though, if you would stay for a little while. We need to catch up."

"What will Julio think? He didn't seem happy to have me here."

"You just leave him to me. I can take care of Julio, in

every way. I want to have my friend around for a while. Besides, you need somewhere to stay, no?"

"Yes, I do. It's getting cold out these nights and it's going to snow soon."

"Then you will stay. Who knows what will happen with the men? Miguel, he likes blondes, so I'm sure he'll like it if you stay!"

"Well then how could I refuse? I guess we're roommates now!"

Sunny hooked her arm through Yolanda's and they walked to the threadbare, flowered sofa in the tiny living room and plopped down together to start catching up.

Chapter Eleven

Miguel was thrilled to have Sunny staying with them because it meant that *he* had someone to woo for once. He didn't dare look twice at Yolanda or Julio would kill him.

He flirted with Sunny every chance he got. But to his dismay, it was the enigmatic, red-haired rebel that Sunny was drawn to.

Raymond paid little attention to anyone else in the house. He was wrapped up in his craft. Making Crystal Methamphetamine was the thing he was best at. He was a chemist at heart and he spent untold hours in the shop tweaking the formula that would process Julio's Mexican-manufactured ephedrine into the perfect rock.

Raymond spent very little time actually getting high. He waited until he had what he thought was the perfect crystal and then he would test it. He believed that smoking the stuff in between would impair his ability to discern good smack from sub-par smack. He didn't have a habit. He had an obsession.

Thus far, Sunny had refused to try the drugs. She didn't want to lose control again like she had done a lifetime ago with Duwayne. She made all kinds of excuses and eventually the others stopped offering. This made Sunny and Raymond the only people in the house who were regularly sober and she found herself thinking about him quite often.

He was the strong, silent type, more inclined to listen than to talk. But when he focused those luminous green eyes on her, Sunny's breath would catch. If he engaged her in conversation, she would blush to the roots of her hair as she stumbled to reply. On occasion he would reach around her to grab a glass or get something out of the fridge and a bolt of pure physical attraction would shoot through her.

She had a bona fide crush and she knew it. The trouble was, Raymond didn't seem to know she existed, except as someone to prepare his meals and share the living room floor with. It was probably for the best that he didn't share her feelings. After all, logic told her, he *is* a drug dealer, however cute.

The only drawback to her new situation, besides the fact that she had very few of her own things, a sleeping bag on the floor instead of a bed, and about one minute of hot water in her shower every morning, was having to listen to all of the obscene noises Julio and Yolanda made through the thin wall of the bedroom every night.

It was no wonder Miguel was so hopeless! They went at each other all night long.

Consequently, the shadows beneath Yolanda's eyes grew deeper and she took to napping during the day while Sunny did more of the chores.

Since she and Yolanda never went anywhere, there wasn't a chance that Gwendolyn or her parents would find her here. The only person who even knew where Sunny had been going was Cassandra and Yolanda had called her to swear her to secrecy.

It was two days before Christmas when Miguel and Julio went to town to get more supplies for Raymond and to get a Christmas tree.

They returned in a panic, without a tree or paint thinner. Sunny could tell by their gestures that something was terribly wrong. Yolanda listened for a few minutes and came over to where Sunny stood watching.

"Yolanda. What's happening?" The men were in conference. Only Raymond appeared to take in the information calmly.

"Miguel went to deliver a package to a customer and found out that another buyer he had been making arrangements with had been exposed as an informant.

"It is only a matter of time until they bust this operation. The cops got a lot of information and they were sniffing around today's buyer too," Yolanda explained, her eyes full of fear.

"What does all of that mean? Will the guys be arrested?"

"All of us, Sunny, even you, we are all involved. They are trying to figure out what to do."

"I could get *arrested*?" She hadn't really thought about that. But she did know about the drug operation and she didn't report it. That made her an accomplice. She'd read enough crime novels to know the truth of the matter.

Julio came over to them.

"Yolanda, you and your friend need to hustle and pack whatever you can out of the house. Load it in the back of the Blazer, pronto. We need to get a head start. We need to leave town within the next hour, so only take things that you know can be packed quickly. Miguel and Raymond and I will have to take what we can still get out of the lab."

Sunny reeled. They were leaving! She had been with this group of people for a month and she knew she was up to her eyeballs in trouble, as they all were. Subconsciously, though, she had always thought that she would return to Gwendolyn's once she could be sure that her grandma was okay.

There was no way to do that if they were going to leave. Where would they go? Couldn't they be arrested anyway, even if no one discovered the lab in the shop? Obviously Julio and Miguel were already under investigation. How on earth was she going to get out of this mess?

All of these thoughts rushed through her mind as she helped Yolanda zip up the house. They packed only the essentials: clothing, blankets, sleeping bags, canned food and paper plates and plastic utensils. They didn't have a whole lot of bags, so they grabbed boxes from around the yard and shop to pack things in.

They packed the back of the Blazer full in just a half-hour. It took Julio, Miguel, and Raymond about forty-five minutes to clear out what they needed from the shop. With that, they were on the road.

Julio took the less-traveled road from the Bar to a small, wheat-producing town at the top of the Columbia Plateau, Mansfield. They went from there to an even smaller wheat town, Hartline, and that's where they ditched the Blazer.

Apparently, Julio knew that his car could be trailed too, so he looked for the first opportunity to get another vehicle. He was on the lookout for a cargo-style van. When they spotted one a few miles west of Hartline at a rural farm, he knew this was their opportunity.

He'd taught his little brother how to hot-wire a car when he was just ten years old, so he dropped Miguel off just a few yards from the farm and continued down the road a few miles to a county gravel pit. Miguel started and took off with the van without incident. They rendezvoused at the gravel pit and transferred the contents of the Blazer to the Chevy van.

They knew that the Blazer would be easily spotted in the gravel pit, so Julio drove it back several miles to where they had seen a small stand of trees surrounding a pond. Thank goodness it wasn't late enough in the year to have frozen the pond over completely.

Sunny watched in amazement as Julio drove his beautiful red car right to the edge of the pond, put it in neutral, exited, and pushed the back of the vehicle until it rolled into the brackish water. Then, cool as a cucumber, he walked over to the Chevy and made Miguel scoot over into the passenger seat so that he could drive.

Looking back through the grimy rear windows, Sunny could see the Blazer sinking and as they hit the road, she could see that the stand of trees, despite their lack of leaves, made a wonderful disguise for the pond's new occupant. It might actually be until the next summer when the pond dried up that their vehicle would be found.

The only trick was getting their get-away car to their next destination before it was reported missing by its owner.

Julio was continually chatting in Spanish with Miguel,

plotting their steps as they made their quick escape. The group continued from Hartline to Moses Lake, where they fueled up. Then they met up with Interstate 90, heading West. Sunny had never been West of the Cascade Mountains in her short life. It looked like she was about to get her first dose of the populated side of the State.

The Chevy, despite its dull, rusted gray exterior and run-down interior, ran like a champ for their journey. They stopped once more for gas just West of Snoqualmie Pass in North Bend. Julio let Sunny and Yolanda go inside to get some hot food. They were all starving, and canned provisions didn't appeal to any of them.

To Julio's dismay, Yolanda wasn't handling the trip well. It had been just over six hours since they had to flee the Bar and he could tell that she was badly in need of a fix. He hadn't realized just how bad her habit had become since he was preoccupied most of the time with manufacturing and delivering the stuff. They needed to get somewhere soon so he could take care of her. Come to think of it, he could use a smoke too. But he dismissed the thought. He needed to keep a clear head if he was going to keep them all from getting caught.

It would be okay, though. Julio had been through this many times before and he was yet to get caught. He was smart and resourceful and had made many allies among other dealers. It was the reason he had come to Washington in the first place. That and Yolanda—she had definitely been part of the decision to leave California. She was his and he was hers. He had never loved anyone like Yolanda.

Freedom had its own benefits, but he would die before he would let them put her away.

He had a friend, Rico, also from California, who had settled his operation into the assistant manager's unit at an apartment complex in Kent. Rico had always been slick—well-dressed, charming, and above reproach for his shady dealings. That was why Julio liked him.

Turned out the manager of the complex only came around a couple of times a year. Rico had the run of the place. He had agreed when Julio called him to put them all up until they could set up another house. They would stay in a two-bedroom apartment next to his. Julio and Raymond would help Rico run his lab and Miguel would do deliveries.

The girls could continue to keep house, though Julio secretly wished the quiet little blond would go away. She cared way too much about his Yolanda. He found that somewhat threatening. He kept her around, though, because Yolanda seemed too tired these days to get much housework and cooking done. They needed Sunny for now. Maybe Miguel would talk her into the sack one of these days, then she'd be doubly useful.

After the girls returned with greasy chimichangas and jo-jo potatoes, they all feasted in the back of the van. Shortly thereafter, they headed South on Highway 18 to Kent, a bedroom community for Seattle that had as many new strip malls as it had apartment complexes.

The weary group straggled into Rico's complex just after dark and he let them into their apartment. They unloaded their stuff and Julio and Miguel, as tired as they were, went to ditch their van, not wanting to chance that someone would spot the license plate. They could get another used car later with some of the money they had brought with them. Rico followed in his yellow Mustang and after they left the van in a dense wooded area about five miles East of town, he took them back to their new home.

Chapter Twelve

A casual observer would never know that the meth operation had ever been moved. That was how quickly Raymond had his lab back up and running alongside of Rico's. To Sunny, life didn't change much from the Bar, except that it rained more. Wintertime in Seattle meant lots of gray, rainy days.

Sunny didn't mind the weather so much, but living in the apartment complex meant closer quarters. They had more room in the apartment than they had in the shack, but now there were neighbors very close by. They needed to appear to be productive members of the community, not sleazy drug dealers.

She and Yolanda tried to keep to themselves, for the most part. As before, the men brought them groceries and supplies. Their apartment, however, did not have a washer and dryer, so they had to take laundry to the central Laundromat in the middle of the complex. Sunny enjoyed going to the Laundromat, because she finally felt like the world was bigger than the four walls of their apartment.

Even Yolanda would perk up and dress and make herself up as if she were going somewhere really important. It was a destination, even if it *was* only a Laundromat. Sunny continually worried about Yolanda and her obsession with drugs and Julio. Even when Sunny had shown her that she had her paints and brushes, Yolanda hadn't been interested at all in painting again. She went so far as to tell Sunny that she couldn't paint either. The men would think she had too much free time and that would be bad for both of them.

Sunny thought she would go crazy with the monotony, the boredom that was supposed to be her new life. There was nothing to read, no painting, no newspapers, and nothing to look forward to.

Things were about to get interesting, though. It was three months into their stay in Kent when, with Spring fast-approaching, Raymond finally made a move on Sunny.

It had almost become a joke between Sunny and Miguel how he kept trying to seduce her and she kept thwarting his efforts. They had become friends and he was very clear on that issue. Raymond observed all of this with detached interest. He was, after all, a young man, and Sunny, though a bit scrawny for his taste, was a wide blue-eyed blonde. She also had a sweet smile if someone could tease it out of her, as Miguel often did.

Raymond hadn't been blind to her school-girl crush. He just hadn't had time in Brewster to notice it. Now with Rico minding the store half of the time, he caught her curious gaze on occasion. He hadn't acknowledged it, but perhaps the impending Spring was influencing him.

One late March day when Sunny was setting his lunch plate down in front of him, Raymond caught her eye with his green stare and, to her complete astonishment, he winked at her and gave her a quick smile.

The butterflies in her stomach beat their giant wings and

she smiled back that brilliant smile. Sure she was underage, but then he was only nineteen, only four years older than her, and they were all living like adults now.

Later that evening, he invited her to sit outside on the concrete steps with him. They didn't really talk much, but he reached out and grasped her hand while they sat there. He first massaged each finger at its middle knuckle and then laced his fingers with hers and squeezed them gently. Not that she had much experience, but she thought it was the most erotic thing she had ever felt, holding hands with the enigmatic Raymond.

Raymond took things slow, not wanting to scare Sunny off, but definitely letting the others know that she was now his girl. He'd taunt her with quick caresses or chaste kisses before heading off to "work" next door. He'd put his arm around her while they all watched rented VHS videos on their 19-inch TV (the only convenience Julio had allowed them since their arrival.)

Raymond respected that Sunny did not want to try Meth, but he did want her to see what an art form he had made of producing it. He finished a particularly potent batch one early April evening and, having tried it himself, in his euphoria, he asked Sunny if she would mind trying it with him.

"Pretty little Sunny, won't you at least try it? I know you don't want to, but it's only just this once. I have produced the perfect crystals. Can't you see? I want you to feel as good as I do. That's all."

"I've seen you all using, but I wouldn't even know where to begin. I'm just a dummy when it comes to a pipe,

Raymond. I can see that you feel really good right now. Would it hurt your feelings if I didn't try?"

"I want you Sunny. I have for weeks now. But I want you when we *both* feel like this. Just try a little. It won't hurt, I swear. Besides, look at me. I only smoke every once in a while and I'm not addicted, am I? That's what you're afraid of, isn't it? That you'll be a junky like Yolanda?"

"Don't talk about Yolanda, Raymond. Yes, she has a problem. We'd be stupid to ignore that. Let's just say that I've lost control before and it got me in a heap of trouble. If I do this, Raymond, it'll be just this once, and it's because I trust you to take care of me."

Just hearing her talk about losing control was exciting him beyond reason. He pleaded, "Of course I'll take care of you. You're my girl. Please, Sunny. Please try my perfect crystal. Do it for me, for us."

Sunny solemnly took the pipe from Raymond and he lit the crystal for her. She inhaled the smoke and it burned her lungs terrifically. After her fit of coughing subsided, Raymond offered her a second hit. She took it more smoothly this time and the world all of a sudden took on crystal clarity.

This didn't just make her feel good or erotic, it made her feel *strong*, like she was a Nordic goddess, all-knowing and all-powerful. She didn't just offer herself to Raymond that night. She consumed him. Or, more appropriately, they consumed each other.

After that, Sunny let the drug into her life with regularity. If Raymond offered, she took. To her, her creativity blossomed while she was using. She could paint better than ever, and to Julio and Rico's dismay, she started to paint elaborate murals on the white apartment walls. She didn't care what they thought. This was her crystal world. She was going to make it beautiful.

Sunny cooked delicious, gourmet-style meals. She kept the apartment neat as a pin and, instead of saving laundry for the end of the week, she did daily loads. The drugs made Yolanda more and more tired and despondent. They made Sunny soar. They made her capable, energetic. Without even knowing or admitting it, Sunny was hooked.

Raymond noticed. But he didn't care. She was willing to come to him whenever he beckoned. Besides, they were producing the stuff, so it wasn't like they couldn't afford the girls' habits.

Even Julio stopped being bothered by Sunny's presence. Raymond was a good man to have around. They had been friends for years now. If having Sunny made him happy, then she could stick around. It was actually pleasant to have her here now that she wasn't being a prude.

The months rolled by. It was an unseasonably warm, dry summer in Seattle. The drug operation was doing very well, and the group and Rico made several outings to explore the area. They went to the zoo in North Seattle and to the open air market in Seattle proper. They checked out the Seattle Waterfront and Pioneer Square. They went to the amusement park and new waterslides in nearby Federal Way.

Sunny, Yolanda, and the men had a great time. Even Miguel got to pick up on a few women. They were a happy bunch, seemingly prosperous and fun-loving. Only a close observer would know that the fun was supercharged. Julio made sure that nobody got that close.

It was Raymond who first noticed that Sunny didn't ask any of the guys to pick up her feminine products in the month of September. Since he made regular trips to the hardware and grocery stores in the area, he waited for her to ask him to pick up her regular supplies. He soon dismissed his suspicion, though, thinking that she probably just had some left from before.

Sunny, who had celebrated her sixteenth birthday faintly missing her family, especially her Aunt Gwen, and then smoking the lonely thoughts away, was too busy painting her murals and cooking exotic meals to notice the absence of her monthly cycle.

When mid-October arrived and, to Raymond's knowledge, she still hadn't gotten her period, he freaked.

"Sunny. We need to talk."

"Baby, we can talk, or do whatever else you want," she smiled sweetly. She was amped, but he couldn't wait for her to sober up to talk about this. It was too important.

"Sunny, you haven't gotten your period in a while. I've noticed."

"So?" She really was clueless.

"So, do you think that maybe the reason is that you're pregnant?"

"WHAT?" Suddenly alarmed and confused, Sunny tried hard to concentrate on what Raymond was saying.

"Can't there be other reasons? When was the last time anyway? I don't remember, do you?"

108

"I just know that you haven't sent me to the store for tampons in a while. Yolanda has, but you haven't."

"But we used condoms. I do remember that."

"Yeah, Sunny, most of the time we did. There were times that we were too excited to get it done."

"There were?" Sunny started to wring her hands together. This was just a bad trip. They weren't really talking about this. One thing was for sure—her euphoria was wearing off.

"Listen. I don't want to think about the possibility of you being pregnant either, but you've got to check it out, okay, Sunny? We need to know."

Raymond was being outwardly calm; inside he was anything but. He was having fun with Sunny, but he wasn't ready for any more than that. He certainly wasn't ready to look fatherhood in the face. He was too young and too busy. There was no room for babies or commitment of any kind.

Sunny was so stunned by Raymond's revelation that she spent the next two hours completely sobering up. Then she walked the five blocks to the nearest grocery store and bought a pregnancy test and a can of cola. She needed caffeine right now, not a fix (though that would make her much calmer, she thought.)

The test she bought would show just one line if she was not pregnant, but two lines if she was. By now, Yolanda and Julio and Miguel were privy to the drama that was unfolding. The whole gang was waiting outside the bathroom door. Sunny was horrified when the second line appeared, almost instantaneously. She reeled. Then she turned around and threw up.

Sunny Moss was sixteen, hooked on methamphetamines, · in love with a devil of a redheaded man, and pregnant with his child. She thought she'd seen trouble before. That was nothing compared to what was on its way.

Chapter Thirteen

At the sound of Sunny's retching, Raymond took it for what it was and turned around and punched the wall right beneath the giant sunflower that adorned it. This was *not* what he'd had in mind when he had taken Sunny to bed. This was her fault. She should have taken the pill or something.

Julio grabbed Raymond by his upper arm and steered him toward the door before he could do any more damage to his hand or the wall. Miguel followed close behind.

Yolanda began to cry softly and knock at the door, begging Sunny to let her in so they could talk. She felt responsible for her friend, since Sunny was with them because of her. She shouldn't have let that shady Raymond even get close to her.

Sunny flushed the toilet and washed her face. She had no tears, just despair and hopelessness. She'd really done a number on herself now. Her mother would say that she deserved it, behaving as she had. She couldn't imagine how Gwendolyn would react. She would be disappointed, surely, but Sunny wished Aunt Gwen was here for solace, nonetheless.

She opened the door and Yolanda flew into her arms. Sunny began to comfort Yolanda, though she needed comforting herself. She noticed that Raymond and the other guys had disappeared. She also noticed a gaping hole in the sheet rock below her garden mural. So he wasn't taking this well either.

She and Yolanda sat together in silence on the living room sofa until darkness fell. As Yolanda got up to flip on the light, Julio and Miguel came through the outside door, looking grim. Raymond had left in the car. Julio said that he needed to clear his head.

All three of them went to the bedroom to take a hit. They offered the pipe to Sunny, but given her news, she felt sickened at the thought of putting more Meth into her body. Much as she would like to forget, that wasn't and wouldn't be the way to do it. Sunny was strong-minded and strong-willed. If she decided she was done with drugs, she would be, painful as it might be.

What she really wanted to do was talk to Raymond. She needed to know how he felt about all of this. Would they get married? Get their own place? Have a family, starting now? The more she thought about it, the more she got attached to the idea of growing this little soul inside of her. She would nurture this child from now forward. No more drugs. No more promiscuity. Only good food and good karma for her baby.

She was totally ill-prepared for the angry, red-faced, drunken man that returned to the apartment at almost midnight. Raymond had been the one to ask about the pregnancy. He had wanted to know. Why was he so *angry*?

"You little slut," he started, "You tricked me into this, didn't you? You had this planned from the minute you

112

started making doe eyes at me."

Sunny didn't know that Raymond came from a family with nine children. He had never planned on having his own kids. He felt like his father had been trapped into having more and more babies by his baby-loving, Catholic mother. There had never been enough food, enough clothing or shoes, or enough love to go around. It had been chaos and he had gotten out as soon as he turned fifteen.

She was thinking much more clearly than he was and with a whole lot less baggage.

"Raymond, I didn't expect this either, obviously, or I wouldn't have been so surprised when you asked me about it. Let's just talk this out calmly, okay?"

"The only way I'll be calmer is if I'm dead. What is there to talk about anyway? You're going to see a doctor and you're getting an abortion. Julio told me he'd pay for it. You just need to find a clinic."

"Are you hearing yourself? I just barely found out that we are going to have a baby and you're asking me to make an appointment to kill it! Why are you being this way? I thought you cared about me."

"I care about me, Sunny, and what I do and I never asked for this kind of trouble. Just get this done, will you?" He was wild-eyed.

Sunny was weary and it was late. She could see that she wouldn't be able to talk to Raymond reasonably until he at least had time to sober up and get some sleep. She would go to a clinic in the morning and get checked out. After that, they would make a decision.

She shrugged a resigned look at Raymond and slipped

into her bed, letting her fatigue carry her to sleep.

There was a clinic just half a mile from their apartment complex, so she called in for the earliest appointment. They were happy to fit her in at two o'clock. She avoided the others as best she could until it was time to walk to the clinic.

Yolanda offered to go with her. Sunny appreciated the offer, but with Raymond being so apathetic about the whole situation, she really just wanted to handle this by herself. It was her mess, her body. She just wanted as much information about her situation as she could get. She didn't feel like she would be free to ask as many questions if anyone else was there to influence her.

She was going to have to come clean about her drug usage. She knew they would ask her about that because it affected the health of the baby. Yolanda would be evasive and defensive if Sunny started answering questions.

Sunny just didn't need the additional stress. She was already dry-mouthed and sweaty and achy and mindlessly bored, all things she assumed stemmed from going cold-turkey. She would not take a fix, though. That was not for her anymore. Control was key and she was reclaiming hers.

Sunny left the apartment at one, giving herself plenty of time to take in the fresh, crisp fall air. She was about halfway to the clinic, waiting for the 'Walk' signal when she looked at the car next to her. It was a late model economy car, silver.

It wasn't the car she noticed first. It was the woman and an adolescent girl who could only be her daughter in the passenger seat. They were singing along to the radio, loudly enough to attract her attention. The song ended and they looked at each other and giggled. They were the only two people in the world—completely unaware that they were being observed.

Sunny suddenly missed her Aunt Gwen. And she longed for a moment like that with her own mom.

The light turned green and Sunny walked a little further. Then she remembered why she was walking in the first place.

She was going to be a mother. Could she have a moment like that with her own daughter? She was sure that she could. After all, she could be a really good mom with some practice. She would love this child with her whole heart and give him or her the world, or at least a piece of it. Her child would never doubt her love, because she would swaddle this baby with it all of the time.

But, she reconsidered, this child would not have a father to love him or her the same way, because Raymond wanted her to have an abortion. One thing that had always sustained her when she thought her mother loved only Avery was that her dad was her own and she didn't have to share him. Could she really bring a baby into the world that only had one real parent, that being a sixteen-year-old hopeless young woman?

Her pondering led her to the clinic lobby. The doctors here were all general practitioners, but they dealt with plenty of teenage moms from the Kent area. This neighborhood especially had a lot of low-income families and uneducated inhabitants. Unplanned pregnancies unfortunately ran rampant here.

The doctor and his nurse were kind and gentle with Sunny, helping her through her first pelvic exam and Pap smear. They asked her many personal, probing questions, all of which she answered honestly.

The doctor looked grim when she talked about her drug use. Hers was a tough situation, oftentimes insurmountable. He'd seen too many young women fail to abstain from drug use during their pregnancies, having premature, underweight, addicted infants, and abandoning them to continue their habits.

What Sunny didn't know was that only about three percent of Methamphetamine addicts actually escaped the pattern of addiction and recovered. What she was expecting of herself was virtually impossible for less strong-willed people. The doctor made no assumptions, just gave her the facts about her situation and what could happen to the baby should she continue using.

If she hadn't been scared before about being a mom, she was terrified now. What if her baby was already damaged by what she'd been doing? She certainly wasn't going to continue to take those risks.

She never actually brought up ending her pregnancy to her doctor, but there was an underlying understanding in their conversation that she hadn't ruled out the possibility.

Sunny needed an ultrasound to determine how far along she was. The minute she saw her tiny, blurry baby bouncing around on the monitor, she knew that she could never terminate this pregnancy. Her baby was real and perfect and already a few months old. She would be due at the end of

116

April.

The technologist gave her a picture and she returned to the clinic where her nurse introduced her to a woman who would help her apply for State assistance with medical care.

Sunny's head was spinning with information and fatigue by the time she left the clinic. She found that she was starving and stopped for fries and milk at a fast food joint on the way home. She sat and enjoyed watching the children dart among the tables, their mothers begging them to settle down to their meals.

She was euphoric. This was going to be fun—an adventure. She could talk Raymond into this, she thought, with more confidence than she felt.

Not only was Raymond unwilling to be talked into anything, the minute Sunny showed him her ultrasound picture, he threw it to the floor and stomped on it. She was horrified, immediately picking it up and smoothing it out the best she could. What if this was the only picture she got of her baby while he or she was inside?

Raymond was furious. He had already made it clear to Julio, Miguel, and Yolanda that Sunny was leaving. Whether she got the abortion or not, she was no longer going to be a distraction for him. His focus was making Meth. He should never have allowed her to penetrate his concentration in the first place.

When she walked into the bedroom to put her picture in a safe place, Sunny discovered that her clothes, toiletries, and paints and brushes had all been placed neatly on the bed. She turned to find out who had done it and found

Raymond standing in the door, holding a beat up duffle bag.

"What are you *doing*? What gives you the right to go through my things?" Sunny was fatigued after her big day. She couldn't believe that she now had to deal with Raymond and this obvious affront.

"I didn't go through them, Sunny. I put them all in one place so that you could pack them quickly and get out."

Tears sprang to Sunny's eyes. He was making her leave! She had expected Raymond to resist becoming a father. This was so much worse than she could have imagined.

"Where am I supposed to go, Raymond? Can't we just talk about this?"

"I already told you how I feel about this. I will *not* be a dad. I'm through with you and your trap. I have things to do, other things to focus on. I don't want you here and Julio and Miguel want me here. I am the key to their production. They need me and none of us need you, Sunny. I guess that means you're out of luck."

"Yolanda needs me. I have to stay to help her keep the apartment. We're friends. That's the reason I'm here in the first place."

"Julio can take care of Yolanda. She was managing just fine before you came. Just take the bag and pack your crap and get out."

"Raymond, *please*. I don't have anywhere to *go*." Sunny dropped to her knees and pleaded with him, tears streaming down her cheeks.

"Get up, Sunny. Julio is willing to give you five hundred dollars, enough to get you an abortion and get you gone. That is it, though. Now leave me alone. I don't want to see you again."

Sunny would never forget the hate in Raymond's eyes as he disposed of her. She had once wanted to drown in those green pools, thinking that she could sink into them and somehow meld with him. And as he turned his back now and sauntered cooly away, Sunny thought that his spiky red locks had turned to fire. Surely hell was where he belonged.

Well, Sunny was not going down with him. She straightened her shoulders and got busy packing.

When she had finished, she exited through the living room. She took the five crisp one hundred dollar bills that lay on the kitchen bar counter. After all, she would need them to get where she was going. Which was *where*? She wondered.

Yolanda, Julio and Miguel sat on the living room sofa. Yolanda was sobbing and she refused to meet Sunny's eyes. The men were in control and they had made their decision. It was time for Sunny to leave.

She stuffed the money in her front jeans pocket, threw the light duffel over her shoulder and defiantly left her old life behind once again.

Part Two

Chapter Fourteen

Sunny Moss had been gone for nearly a year and no one in the Okanogan had heard from her. She had completely disappeared the night of her grandmother's injury.

Sunny would have sworn that her family didn't care about her absence and that they were better off without her around causing trouble. She knew they wouldn't be looking for her.

Sunny could not have been more wrong.

Gwendolyn Mota had been forced to deal with her mother's horrible hip fracture the night of Sunny's disappearance. She had comforted Margaret the best she could and talked lengthily to her doctors. Her mother would require surgery to repair her hip and would need short-term twenty-four hour nursing care while she recovered. This would require a nursing home for at least a few months.

She absorbed and accepted all of this news. She listened to her mother rant about her 'no-good niece' and the trouble she had caused. She slept fitfully that night in an uncomfortable vinyl-covered chair in the corner of her mother's room.

And she worried the entire time about Sunny. When Margaret had been taken on the ambulance, Gwendolyn had called Patty and Gus and had them go by the house to check on their daughter on their way to the hospital. She, of course, was nowhere to be found. Gwendolyn had no choice but to postpone her search for Sunny because of Margaret's immediate medical needs.

As soon as Margaret was out of surgery and on her way to recovery, the Mosses and Gwendolyn began to search for Sunny in earnest. Gwendolyn's first thought was to contact Yolanda. She had been Sunny's only good friend in her year in Brewster. But Yolanda's grandmother, as upsetting as it was to her, didn't know where Yolanda was.

The local authorities listed Sunny as a runaway as soon as they learned her history. They would be on the lookout for her, but they warned her family that it would be a daunting task to find a girl so troubled, who obviously didn't want to be found. If she had been kidnapped, the search for her would have been swift and vigorous. Unfortunately, the effort to find her would rest almost entirely with her family because she was obviously a runaway.

When months of asking and looking and wondering turned up no clue as to Sunny's location, Gwendolyn gave in to despair. Her mother's recovery had been slow and arduous. Margaret was still in the local nursing home. She was even more bitter and intolerant than previously. She made it clear that Sunny's absence was a good riddance in her eyes.

Gwendolyn went to see her mother less and less. Her search for Sunny became an obsession. She called and mailed pictures to local police and hospitals all over the State, hoping that someone would recognize her niece.

She went on with her work, but spent most of her lonely evenings driving aimlessly around the County, hoping that she would see Sunny's face in some random place nearby.

By coincidence, Gwendolyn did run into Miguel and Julio at the Brewster Drugstore and recognized Miguel as one of the thinners who had worked with Sunny the previous summer. She felt a faint glimmer of hope that they might know Yolanda's whereabouts and lead her to Sunny. When she approached them, they told her they were in a hurry and left without giving her any information.

Gwendolyn couldn't have known that was the very day that Julio's whole group would flee the area. Her chances of finding Sunny went from slim to none. The only daughter she had ever known was lost to her. Gwendolyn didn't know how she was ever supposed to live with that.

Patty, at first, was angry with Sunny for causing Margaret's devastating injury. She bought her mother's story, blaming Sunny for her fall and leaving her for dead. As more time went by, though, and it appeared that they might really lose Sunny for good, Patty's anger turned to regret.

Suddenly it didn't matter what Sunny had done over the years. She was her one and only daughter and Patty had abandoned her time and time again. She began to see how she should have shown Sunny love and understanding when she made trouble. She should have never allowed Sunny's physical and verbal abuse. She now understood that she'd done it for attention, something Patty hadn't given Sunny enough of.

It was Avery who made her see it. He had been home for spring break and he, too, was deeply concerned for his only sister. She had been a royal pain in his ass all of these years, but he loved the scrawny little runt. She had deserved a good whipping now and then, but she didn't deserve to have her parents abandon her and then, ultimately, to become a runaway.

Avery had been skeptical of Patty's plan to have her sister finish raising Sunny. He had told his mother all along that she should give Sunny another chance. Even when fully informed of her transgressions, Avery still thought that her actions had been those of a stupid kid, crying for help and he urged his mom at the time to reconsider. Patty wouldn't hear of it.

While he was home for his break, he finally let Patty have it.

"You can't give up on finding her, Mom."

"I haven't given up, Avery. I just don't even know where to start trying to find her. Sunny is responsible for this. She is always the one who makes her own problems. We are just on the sidelines, forced to watch her destroy her life."

"Mom. I love you. But I'm going to tell you something. I'm an educated man, now. I know I'll always be your little boy, but I've learned a few things about people these last few years.

"Kids are never solely responsible for the bad things that they do. Parents and their influence, good or bad, are also a big factor in a child's poor decisions. Let me put it to you this way, Mom. If I had gotten drunk and bedded a girl while I was in junior high, would you have sent me to live with your sister?"

"You wouldn't have done that, Avery. You were a good kid. It would never have occurred to you to do such a thing," Patty replied.

"Mom, I was no angel, believe me. I was just careful not to get caught."

Patty gasped. "Maybe I don't want to hear this."

"You need to, Mom. Most of the time I chose the good and right path, but that was because I knew that you loved me and believed that I would do the right thing. Besides, I wanted to show up old Gus and be the light of your life," he grinned.

Patty smiled back.

"But you never believed in Sunny that way. She was a whiny, demanding little kid. And her dad doted on her, so you thought you could just focus your attention on me and Sunny would make her way."

"That's not true, Avery. I always loved you both equally. Yes, Sunny was hard to deal with, but I kissed and hugged her. She knew that I loved her," Patty was indignant.

"Think about it, Mom. Did you really ever love Sunny without abandon, without judgment? I don't remember when you ever did. I honestly don't. I watched her long for your attention. I watched her big eyes cloud with disappointment when you would gloss over the good things she had done and point out the trouble she made. I watched her regularly devise her next plot to make you miserable. At the time I thought she was just a brat. I've learned since that she needed more from you.

"The truth is, you would *never* have sent *me* away

124

anywhere. She's still a kid, Mom. And she needs you to be her mom, not to judge her. If we ever find her, you need to remember that."

Patty's eyes filled with tears. Avery was right. How could she have been such a terrible mother to her youngest child? She needed another chance with Sunny. Her mistakes had been many, but she would make up for it, if only she got another opportunity. She prayed that her daughter was safe and that she would get her chance.

Gus was the most profoundly affected by Sunny's disappearance. Suddenly the last member of his biological family was gone. They didn't know if she was hurt, if she was staying warm and dry, if she was even alive.

He felt as bereft as he had when his whole family had died in that car accident. Truth be told, he had spent most of his adult life trying to drink away the pain and guilt that went with knowing you were the only one left behind. They had died coming to watch him play football. It was all he could do to live with that. No one could accuse him of having handled that knowledge well.

True, Gus had a regular job. He had a house, a wife, and their two kids. To most anyone, he appeared typical, normal even. But Gus knew, as did his family, that he was a functional alcoholic and that without his beer and his life at the bar, he could not survive.

It took losing his only child to make him admit this to himself. By Christmas, Gus was no longer spending his evenings at the bar. He would simply buy a six-pack on the way home and down it along with his dinner in front of the television. Patty welcomed his company and tried to ignore his continued drinking.

By March, Gus was drinking just two beers in the evening and it seemed to Patty that he was struggling with his ability to limit himself. But she saw that he was trying to beat a long-time addiction and she showed him all of the love and support that she could. At her gentle prodding, by June, Gus agreed to start going to Alcoholics Anonymous.

By August, Gus Moss was completely sober. He had the courage to tell Patty that they had been wrong to send Sunny away. She had realized this herself months before, but it was a refreshing change to have Gus express his opinion regarding their family. He needed her to know that he hadn't ceased to care about them, he had just sunk to thinking that his view didn't matter. After all, who would take the drunk barfly seriously? Sobriety was giving him back his nerve and his good health.

Gus convinced Patty to join the local health club with him. He had once been a competitive, talented athlete. They decided they could both benefit from getting back in shape. They joined the racquetball circuit and spent most of their fall weekends playing in tournaments around the area. It was a great diversion.

By the time Sunny was leaving Kent, her family was losing hope that they would ever find her. But they still longed to see their Sunny-girl. They all moved on the best they could.

Chapter Fifteen

Sister Ellen awoke with a start from her vivid early morning dream. She had been chasing someone down a long, dark alley, sensing that the person was in trouble and in need of help and guidance from her. She'd been startled awake when the alley suddenly opened up into daylight and a transit bus rushed past, barely missing her in her rush.

Sister Ellen felt out of breath and sweaty, unsettled that she hadn't caught up to the person she had been pursuing. Since she was a small girl, Sister had believed that every dream had meaning, some message that needed to be stored for later and analyzed.

She had become a nun because of a dream she'd had when she was twelve. She still remembered the dream very well. She had been an old woman, alone, a spinster with a cold, cynical heart and a young man had knocked at her door. He was tall, slim, with long, flowing, dark hair and a mustache and well-trimmed beard to match. She remembered that her old woman self had needed to squint because the young man was so beautiful, with an obviously kind and peaceful spirit. He was ethereal. He said nothing, just smiled a knowing and forgiving smile, and embraced that decrepit old woman. She felt herself melting, her bitter, old heart unclinching, and the love flowing between herself and the young man.

She knew when she woke that the young man was the Father, and the Son, and after an intermittently attended-to Catholic upbringing, she finally understood the meaning of the Holy Spirit. She believed from that day forward that He had meant for her, Ellen Ryan, to serve Him. He had come to her in her dream to show her what her life would be without faith, and what she could be if she embraced God.

Sister Ellen was all about faith. But she was also an unusual, progressive nun, who believed that there was a little something to palm and Tarot card reading, and she did dabble quite a bit in the interpretation of dreams. As much as she believed in God's goodness and light, she also firmly believed that Satan existed and acted in the lives of God's children. It was her job to deliver them by any means given.

Sister had attended Loyola Marymount and Stanford University and earned Master's degrees in Theology and Fine Arts. She was a fixture at Seattle University, well known there for her work at Campus Ministry and as a moderator on the freshman all-women's floor of the Campion dormitory. She was known citywide as the nun who interpreted dreams on the radio, answering to callers who wanted to know what their dreams meant.

She sat frustrated this morning as she tried to figure out what her own dream had meant. Was God meaning for her to look after somebody special, someone who might be eluding her notice? She would have to pay more attention. Perhaps she would revisit the dream again tonight, but for now she would have to get busy preparing to meet with the Dean of the School of Fine Arts.

She was to be a consultant for the fine art sculptures to be placed in the new student quadrangle. The Dean, Dr. Serena Fetter, was a fellow member of the committee and someone who shared her passion for beautiful paintings and unusual sculpture. Sister had always loved sketching herself, but had never had the aptitude for creating the art that she admired so much. Her drawings were accomplished, but applying paint had proved daunting, so she had stuck with learning about art, rather than creating it.

Sister hurried to her meeting and then to her eleven a.m. radio spot at KUZY. She lunched at the Student Union Building and rushed over to the Lemieux Library to research a few of the artists she and Serena had discussed that morning. She was pleased to note that one of them, after a measurable amount of success, had also become quite a philanthropist. Perhaps he would be willing to donate one of his magnificent copper and epoxy sculptures to the University.

She was high with the effects of a busy, productive day, and getting ready to leave the library when she noticed a young girl who appeared out of place in the periodicals section of the student-filled library. It wasn't her manner of dress that attracted Sister Ellen's attention. After all, this was Capitol Hill in Seattle. The bohemian, baggy-layered look that the girl had was not unusual to this liberal campus. Sister herself preferred loose-fitting, colorful clothing most times, in lieu of her Nun's Habit.

It was her face. The girl was young—too young to be a student at the University, Sister was sure of it. There was occasion for one of the students from the nearby Seattle Preparatory or O'Dea High Schools to be allowed to do research at S.U. But Sister would bet the bank that this girl was not one of them. She seemed sort of unkempt— her blonde hair pulled hastily back into its ponytail, the fingernails of her slim hands dirty and unmanicured.

Sister Ellen moved closer, curious as to why she was in this particular place. She noticed that the girl's coat was ill-fitting through the shoulders, but stuffed through the middle with what she assumed was many layers of clothing for warmth. It was mid-January. Seattle had relatively moderate temperatures in the winter—it rarely froze—but the rainy season made it necessary to keep bundled up to avoid getting chilled.

The girl seemed wrapped up in whatever she was reading. Her brow furrowed with concentration and she scarcely noticed anyone else in the library—until Sister Ellen got just a little too close. She looked up suddenly, startled to see a middle-aged, graying brunette, colorfully attired woman staring at her intently. She barely took the time to register the woman's warm, chocolate brown eyes, realizing that she was not really supposed to be there. She looked for the opportunity to flee.

The girl's wide blue eyes sung her guilt to the nun, but Sister didn't approach her to chastise her. She was only curious about the youngster and why she happened upon this library in the middle of an open, but well-perimetered campus.

"Child, don't look so afraid. I only want to ask you some questions. You look ready to bolt for the hills," Sister smiled her trademark kind, knowing smile.

"I'm sorry, Ma'am. I just realized that I have to be somewhere," thinking quickly, she added, "Classes. You know how it is."

"Of course, dear," seeing that she was lying, but knowing that she would do nothing to further frighten the girl, Sister Ellen let her pass. She muttered under her breath, "Go with God, Child. Go with God."

She turned around to see what periodical the girl had been studying so intently, sure that it would be one of these silly gossip magazines. She was surprised to see that the magazine tossed carelessly on the library chair was not one of these. Indeed it was not gossip. It was the "American Journal of Obstetrics & Gynecology."

"What in the *world*?" Sister Ellen knew then that she was going to have to find this girl again and get to the bottom of this.

Sister Ellen dreamed again that night of the person fleeing her, praying that God would let her see the face before the evil that lurked took that person away again. Her dream took her to a dilapidated, Colonial-style house, all peeling paint and taped-together windows. It looked to be converted into apartments.

The person didn't run up the stairs to the outer door, as she was expecting. Instead, the runner rounded the side of the house. Quickly, Sister darted around the side, just in time to see a cellar door opening and then slam shut.

Sister awoke with a sharp intake of breath as haunted blue eyes awoke her. Just before the door had slammed, she had seen it—the face of the girl from the library!

Sister's heart thrummed with fear for the girl. Something dangerous was pursuing her, with as much determination as she herself had. Sister felt it.

She looked at the clock: Four a.m. She groaned. Today would be a busy day, but she wasn't ready for it yet.

"Okay, God, I hear you. I shall find her. You have my word and my faith that you will help me."

With that, she lay her head back down and tried to find sleep for just a few more hours.

Chapter Sixteen

Eileen Westfield and Shirley Foster had been running the *Fat Cat Tales* used bookstore for two years now. They felt as connected to their neighborhood as they did to the myriad of lazy, colorful cats who lounged around on the walkways and bookshelves they had built for their enjoyment.

Capitol Hill is a neighborhood of contradictions—misfits and yuppies alike prowl its streets. What they seek is cozy cafes with outstanding java, burger joints with as much flavor in the people as the food, and retail stores with a penchant for finding and selling the extraordinary. What they often find is all that and a friendly, urban neighborhood where they can drive around with the windows of their cars rolled down and find conversation at almost every turn.

They can also watch talented musicians playing outside the Broadway Market, get their bodies pierced just about anywhere, dye their hair electric blue, or watch a guy feed French fries from Chip's to his gigantic lizard.

Broadway, the main street through Capitol Hill, is jovial, an attractive place for couples of all kinds, races, and sexual orientation. Those who live and work there are as liberal as a Naked Gay Parade, but as sweet as the chocolate colas at *Shuttle Burger.*

Fat Cat Tales, situated on a side street intersecting Broadway, was as much a part of the culture as the other myriad shops and eateries. People could come there to look for books and read on any one of the numerous inviting couches or intimate tables. They could order a coffee or drink the one that they brought. As long as they didn't mind sharing space with the cats, Eileen and Shirley let them relax however the moment dictated.

Despite and perhaps because of this liberal attitude, the women did a steady business, supporting the store and a lovely, redecorated apartment above, which had not one cat in it. Shirley was actually mildly allergic, so they kept their living space free of felines, but then they had plenty of them downstairs.

Eileen was the cat nut. She had always been surrounded by cats. Her household growing up had too many to count. And when she and Shirley met and fell in love, they agreed that Eileen could have one, as long as it didn't share their bed.

That had been in San Francisco, where they had both attended the University of San Francisco, traveling in separate circles—Eileen, proud president of the Gay and Lesbian Club and Shirley, student manager of the school bookstore and still deep in the closet about her sexuality.

The opposites had attracted at an off-campus party where Shirley had reluctantly agreed to go when her friend Connor had wanted moral support approaching a girl Shirley thought was way out of his league. It turned out that Eileen had similar intentions for the girl. The four of them

134

ended up having a good laugh about it and Eileen, noticing the quietly beautiful Shirley, changed her focus to coaxing her out of her shell.

Twenty-five years later, Eileen and Shirley still had the kind of relationship that gay and straight friends alike admired. Shirley's grace buffered Eileen's bold, in-your-face attitude. They communicated with a glance, with a smile, and with only occasional cross words. They were, in short, best friends, companions, and extremely ordinary lesbians.

There was an aura of sadness about them as well and only those few who had gotten close to them since their move to Seattle knew why.

They had loved San Francisco. Eileen had completed a Master's degree and joined an architecture firm. Shirley had become the manager of a brand new bookstore in the heart of downtown. They had found a steal on an old Victorian at the edge of a rough neighborhood and they and many neighbors had improved their properties enormously into a lovely, historic collection of homes.

When Shirley turned thirty-five, her biological clock started ticking loudly enough for the heavens to hear. Eileen agreed. They needed to have a child in their life before both of them were too old to do so—she wasn't going to be the "mommy." She would be the "daddy." It was the only role she was cut out for.

A semi-anonymous donor, chosen randomly from a group of gay friends, who had agreed to help their insemination, gave them the needed sample. Thus, with a turkey baster, a whole lot of well-wishes, and, yes, prayers,

Shirley and Eileen attempted to have a child.

It took three tries, but they succeeded. Their beautiful, bouncing, eight-pound boy arrived just in time for Christmas. He had Shirley's soft, chestnut eyes and hair and dimples the size of the Grand Canyon. Eileen joked that he had her chin even though they weren't biologically connected. They were completely in awe of this boy, whom they named Garrett Foster Westfield.

Their lives had been wonderful before Garrett, but he quickly became the icing on the cake. With every smile and coo and finally "mamas" and "bye-byes," he wrapped their lives in a cocoon of love.

He grew fast and before they knew it, Garrett was preparing to go to school. They took him for a routine well-child visit at age four, where he would get his necessary immunizations. It was at that doctor's visit and the two that followed that the bottom fell out of Shirley and Eileen's world.

The doctor was concerned that Garrett's spleen was too large. Also he was showing signs of anemia. He ordered a blood test. One blood test led to another and another specialist and then they heard the words that no parent should ever have to hear—Garrett had leukemia. He would need several rounds of aggressive chemotherapy and then they would see.

And see they did. By the time Garrett was seven, he had been in remission twice. Then the leukemia had returned in full force. Shirley had quit her job at the bookstore so she could homeschool him, because he had missed so much being ill. Still, through it all, Garrett had been the smiling, happy boy that they loved. Always positive, always sure that he would get well and never faltering in the belief that God would take care of him.

They learned when Garrett was just barely eight that he would need a bone marrow transplant. They found through research that the best place on the West coast to receive the treatment was in Seattle at the Fred Hutchinson Cancer Research Center. Eileen took a leave of absence from her job and Shirley and Eileen took their precious boy to the Emerald City.

Once there, doctors and nurses stripped Garrett of every ounce of immunity he had left and went to work introducing healthy cells that his mother had been able to donate into his bone marrow.

Then he got an infection, and another. Their world tilted once again, as the two grasped Garrett's frail hands, touched his precious, round face, serene despite his illness, and watched him give his last breath to the world as he went back to the God he so loved and trusted.

Bereft, Eileen and Shirley couldn't go back to the life that they had shared with their son. It was too painful. There were too many reminders. They went back to San Francisco long enough to put their Victorian on the market and sell most of their belongings.

They returned to Seattle and found the old retail space with an apartment off Broadway on their second day back. They fixed up the bookstore, but not too much, wanting it to retain its "used" feeling. They decided to give refuge to several neighborhood cats because Garrett would have wanted to do it. It just tortured him that he couldn't have a cat with his illness because he had inherited Eileen's love for the critters. *Fat Cat Tales* was born out of heartbreak and hope and two years later, they were proud of the role it was taking in their new neighborhood.

They kept a picture of a smiling, healthy Garrett on the wall above the register. When people would inquire about it, the women would share stories about that sweet boy, but they would never talk about the end. Strangers didn't qualify to know.

Then one stranger saw that picture and painted his face on a flat, smooth stone and surrounded it with a field of wildflowers. She never asked about the boy, simply laying that magnificent portrait on the counter and asking if she could take a few books on art in exchange for the rock painting.

Shirley's eyes filled with tears. Eileen had gone out to the Market that day. She knew that Eileen would never have shared Garrett's story with this complete stranger, but Shirley felt that she needed to.

The girl, bedecked in all sorts of layers of clothing, though February sometimes required it, looked every inch the transient that she was. She was grimy and her smell was ripe. She was young with a blond ponytail and blue eyes that told of a wisdom rare for someone of her age. She was thick around the middle and had full cheeks. She didn't *look* like she was starving, but since she was trading rocks for books, Shirley offered her a cup of the hot soup she had behind the counter in a crockpot.

And she told the girl about Garrett, and herself, and

Eileen, and about the bookstore and how it came to be. The girl listened intently, as if knowing that Shirley simply needed someone to listen to her. And her eyes filled with sympathy as she told the girl about their last day with their son. When Shirley was finished, she stopped talking, waiting to see how the girl would take it all in.

The girl nodded and embraced Shirley, smelling of the streets and acrylic paint.

Then she said, "Thank you for the soup, ma'am. I love your little shop and all the books and magazines. I'm wondering if it would be okay if I sold a few of my rocks outside on the sidewalk. I've painted quite a few and I could use the money if I sold them."

It was the most Shirley had heard her say. She couldn't refuse the request. Besides, Eileen would never mind having a girl sell rocks. She let the musicians play outside on a regular basis. Why not have her?

"I've told you my life story and I don't know a thing about you! What's your name, honey?"

"Sunny."

"That suits you. Well, Sunny, it looks like you have some rocks to sell. Just promise me that you'll stop in once in a while for soup and conversation, okay?"

"Okay. Thank you, ma'am."

"Oh, I feel centuries old when you call me ma'am. Call me Shirley."

"Okay, Shirley. I'll come back tomorrow."

And with that the girl with the painted rocks set up shop for the next few months outside *Fat Cat Tales*.

Years later, long after she was gone, Eileen and Shirley would still talk about her—their Sunny girl—and the gift that she would so generously leave behind.

Chapter Seventeen

It seemed to Sister Ellen that the months of January and February passed in a blur. Between the radio show and her obligations at Campus Ministry and the adorning of the quadrangle, she had been busy enough. Now, though, she was also trying to scour the neighborhoods surrounding the University for the gray apartment building she knew from her dream.

Sister didn't drive. Buses traveled much too fast to allow her to examine the sides of buildings for a root cellar. So Sister set about trying to find the building on foot. She covered several miles a week. While she found the exercise stimulating, she was tired of getting soaked to the bone and never finding the old house she was looking for.

She had half hoped that she would run into the girl during one of her walks. But Seattle is a big city. How could she expect to run across a particularly small fish in such an ocean?

It was early March and a beautiful sunny day and Sister had just finished a meeting with the planning committee for the Annual Spring Search Retreat. She was invigorated by the spirit of the young people in the group and by the weather itself. It occurred to her that she should be spending her energy on further search for the girl.

But she was tired of looking. She had made a promise to God about this girl. She knew that she would search more. Her dreams were becoming more and more vivid and the face of the girl more and more terrified. She had to find the girl. She just couldn't bring herself to do it today. The good work would have to wait.

She had to run to the market and get a few things for the girls' night her floor's resident assistant had planned that evening. She also wanted to look for a new pair of sandals to accommodate the changing weather. Her old pair was much too worn to survive another year.

Her shopping could be accomplished by a quick trip up Broadway, just blocks away from the University. She set out along 12th Avenue and walked purposefully toward the side street that she knew would take her by *Fat Cat Tales*. She hadn't been by to see her friends Eileen and Shirley in a while. She had met them shortly after they established the bookstore. She took a stray tabby that had been frequenting the Campus Ministry building to them, hoping to find him a home.

They had taken in the hefty feline, whom they dubbed "Soup," because of his ability to know when the lid was off the crockpot. He would come galloping full speed if he thought he might get a taste of its contents.

They had also befriended Sister Ellen with their ease and hospitality. She saw in *Fat Cat Tales* a neighborhood haven—a place where anyone could relax and feel right at home. She looked forward to going by there today so she could pick up a book that she had heard of at the University about the afterlife and reincarnation, written from a

Christian perspective.

As Sister approached, she noted that the doorway of *Fat Cat Tales* was particularly busy that day, with a duet performing *a cappela* at the east end of the entrance and a girl sitting on a blanket at the west end of the entrance.

She passed the performers with a smile and a dollar for their collection. She glanced down at the girl selling what appeared to be painted stones as she went to pull open the shop door.

She froze with her hand in mid-air when she realized who the girl was. It was her dream-girl, looking very much as she had in the library in January, except that she noticed her face was fuller. She was still dressed in many layers of clothing and Sister imagined that she must be positively cooking on such a warm spring day.

Sister Ellen withdrew her hand from the door handle and stood in front of the girl.

"Do you remember me, child?"

Sunny tried to place the colorfully dressed woman. She looked at home off Broadway, with a silky tie-died caftan and baggy, gauzy pants. Her hair was pulled off her face by a purple bandana scarf. There was something familiar about the eyes. *The library*, she thought with sudden alarm. Surely the woman hadn't come to scold her. She had only been trying to find information about the baby and she had left right away. It wasn't like she had tried to steal back into the library.

Sister Ellen watched familiarity and a flash of fear enter the girl's eyes. Then she saw an edge of defiance there. So the girl had spirit, did she?

"You *do* remember me. We were never properly introduced. I'm Sister Ellen Ryan." She held her hand out for Sunny to take.

She was a *nun*? Sunny hesitated and then held out her own grimy hand. "I'm Sunny. It's nice to meet you," she said politely, dropping her eyes in sudden embarrassment as the nun continued to examine her.

"My goodness, girl, your hands are filthy! Is that from working with the rocks? I know when I spend a lot of time sketching, I end up with charcoal under my fingers that I swear will never come off."

"You draw? I'm much better at painting than drawing."

"I'm the other way around. I see here, though, that you do beautiful work. I particularly like the kale paintings on these rocks here," she pointed to the group of purple green cabbages in the corner. "You make them look so real, so smooth, like the plant itself."

"I love kale. I had to ask the florist at the market what they were. We don't grow those where I come from, so I had never seen one before."

So she wasn't from Seattle and she was a budding artist and entrepreneur. Sister had to find out more—like why she obviously wasn't bathing.

"Well I can see that you are very familiar with sage brush and coyotes and wild sunflowers. You have a talent for capturing them. Are you from the desert?"

"Sort of," not wanting to reveal too much to this complete stranger, Sunny changed the subject. "Do you work at S.U.?"

"I do. I've a job at campus ministry and on the radio and

as a moderator to girls just a little older than you. Do you know that I like to interpret dreams? It is one of my favorite pastimes."

Sunny was a learner, so she was naturally curious about this obviously intellectual woman.

"How do you go about learning how to interpret dreams? Do you just know, or do you have to study?"

"A little of both, I think," Sister replied. She wasn't one to beat around the bush, so she added, "I've been dreaming about you since I saw you, you know?"

Sunny's eyebrows rose in surprise.

Sister continued, "I must tell you that the Lord is telling me to protect you from something. I've sensed that there is some danger lurking about you. To be quite honest, it's the reason I have been trying to find you for the last two months. I'm meant to help you, somehow."

Sister couldn't have known that the girl she was talking to had been offered help at many turns in this journey to Capitol Hill. The clinic in Kent had wanted to help her explore abortion options immediately after she'd been kicked out. She'd fled to Seattle to see if more resources would be available to her there. The women's shelter had wanted to help, but because she was a minor, they had referred her to a social worker, who had tried to persuade her to call her parents.

She couldn't handle the disappointment she was sure would come from her estranged family if they were to know her situation. So she asked for a different caseworker and got a guy this time. He didn't suggest she call her parents, but he was just a little too friendly, putting his arm

around her, rubbing his hands up and down her arms—
Sunny was not stupid and she could tell the guy wanted her
to be easy prey.

By her second week in Seattle, she had decided to leave
the shelter system and try to survive on the meager money
Julio had given her. It hadn't lasted long, though.

She had made her way to soup kitchens out of sheer
hunger and desperation. The workers there wanted to
help with clothes and food, which was fine, but then
someone would eventually get nosey because she looked
so young and so alone. They wanted to send her back to
the bureaucrats that she had fled in the first place. They had
convinced her of one thing: She was making this journey to
motherhood by herself. Anyone else caused completely too
much trouble.

And Sunny was doing fine. She was catching an
occasional meal at the St. James Cathedral Soup Kitchen,
where they had been at least reasonably unmeddlesome.
She had shelter over her head every night. She had
adequate food and drinking water.

She could feel her baby moving night and day. She was
sure that the little tike was safe and sound in her womb.
She had kicked her drug habit, hardly even thinking of her
days as a junkie any longer. She was making a meager,
but sufficient amount of money selling her painted rocks.
Sunny was just fine on her own.

Only one little thing bothered her: she wasn't sure where
she was going to have the baby. But she was sure she could
make her way to any hospital when the time came. They
couldn't turn her away at that point. In the meantime, she

just did her best to make sure she and the baby survived.

Sunny thought a lot about this little person inside of her. Would she have fiery red hair and impossibly green eyes—eyes that she couldn't forget no matter how much of her hated Raymond for putting her in this position? Or would he be sweet and happy and blue-eyed and blond, every Moss gene dominating? Her mom had said that she'd been a fussy, demanding baby. Was she doomed to have the same?

She didn't know, but she was increasingly excited to find out. The baby was her secret, hidden beneath volumes and layers of clothing and he or she was her reason for being good, for staying straight, and for existing. This baby made her *matter* in this great big world and she was going to be his or her champion for the rest of her life.

She unconsciously rubbed toes that were currently assaulting her ribs. She saw Sister Ellen's eyes narrow in on the motion. This woman could only mean trouble for them. Sunny was sure of it. She decided to evade, but subtly.

"Wow. You sure sound convinced that I need your help, Sister. I will have to be more careful, won't I?"

Sister didn't waver.

"I *have* it, Sister!" Sunny tried a different tact, "God wants you to buy my rocks! That would be a great way to help me out! They're only three dollars apiece, two for five dollars. What do you think?"

Sister Ellen had seen the lid slap shut on Sunny's open curiosity the minute that she had noticed the girl rubbing her side. Sister was a perceptive woman. She probed people's dreams and fates, but she never did so if it made them uncomfortable. This conversation about the girl's safety would have to continue later. She could rest with the fact that at least she knew how to find her.

"You must be right, Sunny. I've always wanted kale plants indoors, but they grow much happier outside. I would love to have a few of your rocks inside so I can at least admire the colors. I'll take two please."

Sister paid for the rocks and went on into the bookstore.

Sunny couldn't have known, hours later, that Sister was still waiting for her to leave. She had stayed at the back of the bookstore reading while Sunny came in for an early evening bowl of soup with Eileen and Shirley. Sunny had never seen Sister leave, but then she had been busy with customers most of the afternoon.

As Sunny lumbered home, her body heavy with pregnancy and a blanket full of rocks, she never sensed the quiet woman a half a block behind her the whole way. As she climbed the long, final hill to her street in the waning daylight and turned left toward the apartment building, she never saw the woman aching to help her with her load.

And as she rounded the side of the building, pulled the grape-leaf ivy back from her door, and retreated to her temporary haven, she never caught even a glimpse of the alarm on Sister's face as she faced the gray apartment building from her dream and realized that this obviously pregnant young girl was living in the root cellar of an abandoned building in a very poor neighborhood. Indeed Miss Sunny did need her protection. Sister Ellen just needed to think how she would go about giving it.

Chapter Eighteen

It wasn't so bad in her cellar. Sunny drowned out the smell of wet earth with the sweet smell of sandalwood candles. She brightened the walls and floor with scarves she found randomly at thrift stores and free rummages. Her bed was made from the cushions of an old couch that had been tossed out behind the neighboring apartment building. She used discarded crates and cardboard to make side tables and her painting table.

The whole room was about ten feet square and it was home, for now and as far as she could tell, it was safe. Nobody had bothered her here.

The pack rat that came around on her second night here had given her serious pause, but she found that if she left him a treat or something he could use for his nest each night, he would leave with the treasure and not explore any further.

There were, of course, no plumbing facilities, which, in her increasingly pregnant state made it difficult when nature called. She just made sure that she didn't drink too much water in the last couple of hours before bed. In the guise of darkness she would sneak out behind the apartment building to do her business right before settling in.

Sunny had never been more appreciative of running

water than she was now. She was thankful for the layers of clothing that kept her rank self from stunning her nose all day long. (At night, when she took some of the layers off, she knew the reality was that she *reeked*.)

She did the best she could to clean up at public restrooms, but showers were just not available on every street corner. And most shop owners who did allow public use of their restrooms were suspicious of anybody who spent an exorbitant amount of time in the restroom. So she just tried to wash up here and there and not take too much time doing so.

Even if she could shower every day, her clothes would still be grimy and sweat-soaked. She swore that pregnancy made a person perspire like a mirror in a steam-filled bathroom. She was *always* hot and her many layers soaked that up. But she couldn't just throw them in the wash. She settled for washing most of her clothes once a week at the Broadway Laundromat. She had to do it real early so that she didn't miss any customers going to *Fat Cat Tales* after nine.

The other problem with living underground was that she had no electricity. She had picked up a small kerosene camp stove at a thrift store, spending money that she could ill afford to spend, but she had to have some way to get her canned food hot.

Thank goodness for her paints and brushes. She had an abundance of most colors when she started her rocks and now she was running short on a few. Lucky for her, she had discovered that the Seattle Community College branch on Broadway had painting classes and that they used disposable pallets. She couldn't believe the paint that would have gone to waste had she not gone to investigate the dumpsters.

One thing was for sure. Sunny had no dignity when it came to survival. She was figuring out this way of living. If she had to be less than clean and scrounge for the few possessions she had, she would do so to insure her own survival.

And the baby—the baby would have everything he or she needed because she was collecting that too. She went around on Sundays, when *Fat Cat Tales* was closed, to all of the soup kitchen rummages and the neighborhood thrift stores, who had boxes of free stuff. She was collecting bottles and tiny little clothes and blankets and burp cloths and she was putting them all carefully into a plastic container, which she had bought new from the dollar store. Once a week she would buy a small package of disposable diapers with some of the money she had earned and were they ever expensive!

She had been subtle collecting these things, not wanting everyone to know who she was collecting them for. She was pretty sure that her secret was safe. After all, who cared whether she was pregnant or collecting baby things for a sister or a girlfriend?

Just that nosey nun—she had noticed, Sunny was positive that she had. But she couldn't hurt them. She knew that Sunny worked at *Fat Cat Tales*, but she would never know where to find her besides that. It shouldn't have mattered, but Sunny had become wary of anybody trying to help her.

Sunny sat thinking about her parents and Avery and her Aunt Gwen as she painted rocks later that evening by candlelight. If you had asked her back in Brewster if she could have painted under candlelight in a windowless dungeon, she would have laughed out loud. But she had gotten nothing but compliments on the work that she was doing. She liked to think that the light in her paintings came from the love that she put into them.

Life was hard right now. She had never imagined that she would have to struggle so to survive and to stay straight. But despite all of that, Sunny was happy, happier than perhaps she had ever been. She had put so much energy into her life here, up at dawn, painting or reading late into the night. She had scraped and starved and scrimped, but she was managing, thriving, and growing.

For the first time in her life, she no longer relied on anyone else to make her happy. There was no whining, no conflict, and no anger. She was never lonely with this little life inside her to share her solitude with. She was darn proud of herself. Sunny never knew her instinct for survival was so strong until she had to live hand to mouth. She was a remarkable young woman and she *knew* that to be true and no one could take that knowledge away from her.

March turned into April and Sunny began to feel restless, worried about delivering her baby and what the two of them would do once he or she arrived. She was, as many women are in the last month, simply tired of existing with all of the extra weight and lack of sleep. It was difficult to even walk nowadays.

It seemed the baby was growing weary as well. While he or she used to drum her insides at all hours of the day, it now seemed the baby had slowed down. The movements were less frequent, but with greater impact—more rolling and stretching than kicking. It seemed like she had been pregnant *forever*.

Sunny realized about halfway into April that Shirley and Eileen were catching on to her pregnancy. They asked pointed questions, trying to find out more about this mysterious little painter that came in for her bowl of soup every evening. Shirley wanted to ask her when her baby was due, but Eileen cautioned her that Sunny might not be talking about it because she didn't want anybody to know. It was obvious from her increasing volumes of clothing that she was trying her best to hide it.

Sister Ellen came by about once a week as well. Eileen and Shirley were thrilled to see their friend so frequently, but Sister made it clear that her visits were to keep tabs on their Sunny girl. The three women talked about Sunny while she sat on her blanket painting. Sister, with the little free time that she had, was watching out for her, just like she'd sworn she would. Eileen and Shirley were supportive, offering backup should Sister need help assisting Sunny.

Sister had been following Sunny home for an entire month and she was so preoccupied with getting her cumbersome body from place to place, that Sunny hadn't even noticed. It wasn't clear to Sister yet how she was supposed to help this girl, but she knew that she would have to at least be in the vicinity when the time came.

So Sister Ellen did her daily radio show and made the

meetings that were required of her, and spent every other waking minute trying to keep track of Sunny. She was as exhausted as Sunny was tired of being pregnant.

Sleep wasn't so easy for her either. She had thought that finding the girl would slow down her dreams about her, but that hadn't been the case. Instead of disappearing, the dreams had evolved. Now she didn't see the apartment building, but a dark hole and instead of hearing the sounds of Spring around her, she heard moans and screams. She would wake up smelling blood and sweat and something sweet and musky that she couldn't place.

It was almost easier not to sleep so she wouldn't have to be so traumatized by her dreams. They did harden her resolve to find a way to help the girl. She just prayed that she would be at the right place at the right time.

Chapter Nineteen

It was Saturday, April twenty-seventh and Sunny had done her laundry first thing that morning, knowing that *Fat Cat Tales* wouldn't open until ten. She had wanted to sleep in a little, but then she woke up at five a.m. feeling energetic and motivated, two things she hadn't felt in a while. She carried her plastic laundry bag back up the hill and sat folding the new baby clothes and blankets she had washed.

She straightened up her abode and decided to kill the rest of her morning reading the book on Plato that Shirley had given her when she had confessed insomnia.

Sunny lifted the door of the cellar and sat on the top step, soaking up the dewy spring sunshine and information about the Greek philosopher. Suddenly she felt an odd stabbing sensation down below. She stood up to see if she could relieve the pressure and felt a warm gush between her legs as her water broke right there and then. At the same time, the first labor pain bent her clear in half.

Panicked, Sunny went to grab the plastic bag that she had packed with necessities to go the hospital. She had to get somewhere and she needed to get there fast. She no sooner reached the inside of the cellar when she doubled over again. It felt like somebody was killing her.

Sunny had read many magazine articles and books about child birth, wanting to be informed the best she could, so now she knew that she had to pause and breathe while she was contracting. She didn't have a watch, but she knew that the two pains that she had just had were very close together. She breathed through the second and grabbed her bag. She got back to the bottom step and another contraction gripped her.

Lord help me, she thought, I'm not going to make it. She had scoped out her situation over the last two months. The nearest hospital was Providence and it was a good ten blocks away to the south and west. The apartment building she was in was abandoned, though she knew that several of the neighborhood dealers used it as a meeting place. She certainly wanted nothing to do with anyone who came near the building. The next building over was slightly newer and there were ten apartments. She might be able to get help if only she could get there.

The pains were coming one right after the other. She would no sooner get ready to move again and she would be split in two once more. She was in big trouble and in way too much pain to work it out. All she could do was breathe and pray as she had never prayed before.

Sister Ellen slept in that Saturday, getting a dreamless, peaceful night's sleep for the first time in a very long time. But she awoke with a start at nine o'clock, knowing that something was terribly wrong. She was supposed to be somewhere.

She checked her calendar and didn't see any engagements for that day, but she couldn't shake the feeling that she was missing something. She had been planning to pay a visit to *Fat Cat Tales* anyway, so she went that direction first. She was a half a block away from the store when she realized that the girl was not sitting on her blanket. In fact, nobody was outside the doorway. She consulted her watch. It was almost noon. Sunny was in trouble. *Hurry*, she thought.

Sister hustled up the hill to Sunny's building, thankful she knew the way so well. She could hear painful moans arising from the cellar as soon as she stepped onto the weedy yard.

Sunny thought she was hallucinating when Sister Ellen descended into the cellar. She was dressed in gauzy light blue, her frock and skirt floating about her as she rushed down the stairs. Maybe she had been wrong about the nun. Maybe she was an angel and God had sent her here to take Sunny away, since she was most certainly dying.

Sunny had been in labor for most of three hours and she had been so gripped by it that she hadn't been able to leave. Sister knew nothing about delivering babies, but she knew with utter certainty that one was going to come today. She just didn't know how soon.

"Sunny, it's me, Sister Ellen."

"Sister. Are you real? Am I just dreaming you here?"

"It's not a dream Sunny. I've come to help you, just like I said I would. Looks like I got here just in time."

Sunny moaned as another pain shot through her abdomen. Sister began to look around for more light than just that from the doorway. She found some candles—sandalwood—the sweet smell from her dream.

"How did you find me?" Sunny was still astounded that Sister was there.

"I followed you, but never mind that. Do you have any water down here?"

"There are gallon jugs of it in the far left corner. I need to get to a hospital, Sister. Can we just go to your car, now?"

"I'm afraid not, Sunny. You see. I don't drive. And you are certainly in no shape to take the bus, not that you could walk the two blocks to the bus stop. I am supposing that you are going to have the baby here."

"*Here?* Sister, I can't even handle the sight of blood. You aren't a doctor or a nurse, are you? We can't do this," Sunny was incredulous.

"We don't have to do much, Sunny. Your baby will determine what happens. If it gets too bad, I can always run for help, but I don't want to leave you now. The pains are very close together, aren't they?"

Sunny doubled over yet again and breathed in short pants like she'd read you were supposed to.

"You could say that, Sister," she replied after the contraction subsided.

"I need to check things out below, Sunny. I'm not sure what to look for, but I'm pretty sure that we'll see a head when the baby's about to come out."

Sunny nodded and waited patiently while Sister washed off her hands with a wet towel. If this was the only help that God was going to send her, then she was going to listen the best she could to the nun.

Sunny had another pain just as Sister was setting up candles near the foot of the bed. She breathed and then told Sister, "The pain is changing so that I feel like I want to push against the pressure."

"That sounds promising. Perhaps it is almost time for our baby to come out!" Sister sounded like she was waiting for cookies to come out of the oven, not like she was about to catch a newborn baby.

Sunny moaned. "Are you going to look?"

"I suppose I need to. Let's see. Oh my, Sunny. I can actually see the shape of your baby's head. He is very close to making his entrance."

"I read somewhere that when you feel like pushing that you have to push." Sunny gritted her teeth as she felt another pain coming on.

"Well, push then, dear. Let's see what happens," Sister maintained her calm demeanor, acting ever-prepared for the baby's arrival, though inside she was terrified at the knowledge that they were about to bring a baby into the world in this dirty, dark dungeon.

Sunny held her breath as the next pain overtook her and pushed herself up on her elbows to get leverage while she pushed with all of her might. It felt right to be pushing like this.

"I can see hair, Sunny! You're doing it! Keep pushing, you brave girl!" Sister encouraged.

Sunny waited while the pain subsided and then just a minute later as the pain gripped her again, she held her breath and with a primal scream that came from deep in her gut, she put all of her strength into the next push.

"I have his head, Sunny! Just one more time and we'll have the shoulders. You are doing great! Keep going."

With that, Sunny put her last effort into the push and out came baby, squirming and screaming into Sister's ready hands.

"It's a girl, Sunny! A girl. You did it!" Sister cried tears of relief as she felt the awesome miracle of the moment.

Sunny was also crying as Sister placed her tiny little daughter in her arms and set about taking care of the umbilical cord and placenta like she knew what she was doing. Thank God for Sister Ellen, she thought, as she held her new daughter to her chest.

How Sister had found everything she needed to take care of Sunny and the baby was beyond her. Sunny had towels and blankets and scissors and everything was completely unsterile, but Sister Ellen washed everything off with water warmed by the kerosene stove. She gathered all of the bloody clothing and towels and placenta and put them together in a triple-layered plastic bag to be disposed of later.

By the time she got the baby and Sunny and herself cleaned up, it was evening and the sun was starting to set. She left Sunny briefly to find a dumpster and contemplate what would happen next.

She returned to find Sunny nursing her baby, which she had done several times. The baby girl seemed to be a natural sucker. She just latched right on and got down to business.

Sister watched them and worried about their future. Surely this was not to be the home of this young girl and her babe. She had to do something more for them. One thing she did know was that tonight they needed to rest. Sunny had to recover some more before she could be moved elsewhere. Sister would watch over the two of them until they could all leave together.

The two women smiled at each other over the suckling baby. They were both exhausted. They could talk things over tomorrow. For now, Sister lay a few blankets out on the floor and, at Sunny's request, set out a small, stale roll for the packrat. Then they all lay down to sleep in a cloak of complete darkness.

Sunny awoke several times during the night to feed the baby. It seemed that her girl was born hungry and continued to feel that way. Sunny didn't mind at all. She felt the miraculous, natural bond of motherhood all the more as she nursed her daughter. They both fell asleep as the baby suckled, snug and warm in their embrace.

Sister was not quite so cozy. Her hard place on the floor reminded her constantly that she wasn't in her own comfy bed. She awoke when Sunny did, concerned that she might need something. She fetched a few drinks of water for her and held the baby while Sunny stepped outside to do her business.

The one advantage of being in the cellar was that daylight didn't intrude on the hours they chose to sleep. But Sunny and Sister Ellen were both early risers by habit and despite their long night, they awoke the next morning just as the sun was coming up.

Sunny was anxious to see her daughter in the daylight. Candlelight hadn't been sufficient to examine every detail of her brand new infant's face and hair and body. She needed to really see her because she had an important task today—this baby needed a name.

She sat on the stairs with the door of the cellar open and unwrapped her daughter one hand, one foot at a time so that she wouldn't get cold. She sat memorizing her slightly upturned, but dainty nose, and her long eyelashes, and her perfect, heart-shaped lips. And she marveled at her hair. She already had an awesome cap of thick, soft hair. Sunny could tell that last night as she first held her. But what she could see now, with morning's first light, was that it was also red as fire.

As if knowing that she was being examined, the baby fixed her gaze on her mother's nearby face and allowed the intrusions into her warm swaddle. She was content and, as far as Sunny could see, she was perfect. She smiled at her baby daughter and bestowed her with a name—Leah Kaye.

Her grandmother Moss had been 'Leah' and Sunny had always loved the name. And 'Kaye,' of course, was her dad's sister. She knew her dad would be proud of this new baby girl. Sunny figured that since she had never gotten to meet his family, she could at least honor them by naming her baby girl after them.

Sister Ellen remained in the cellar, giving Sunny privacy with her baby. She watched them, wondering at the invisible strings that tied a mother to her child. This girl was a natural. Age had nothing to do with her obvious ability to bond with her child. It took a while before Sunny announced her name out loud and Sister waited patiently.

She simply nodded her approval when Sunny came back in from the steps and introduced her to 'Leah Kaye.' It was a beautiful name for a lovely little girl.

"Well, Leah Kaye, I guess it's time for your mommy and I to talk about where we go next. Your Auntie Ellen is certainly not going to let you stay in this cellar much longer."

Sister met Sunny's eyes. "I have an idea, Sunny. I have somewhere safe for you two to go if you will let me help you. Please say that you will let me help you."

"Two days ago I would have said 'no,' Sister. I have had so many people try to help me, but there's always a price involved. But you brought my baby girl into the world, Sister. You came for me despite my every effort to ignore you. You helped me when I needed you the most. And now you want to help us more. I can't even begin to thank you for what you've already done."

"You don't have to thank me, Sunny. I started doing God's work a long time ago. He sent me to you. All you need to do is let me help you once again."

"I'll do anything you say, Sister. I trust you. Leah and I need your help. Just tell me what to do."

"I am delighted to hear you say that. I have an idea. Just let me work things out. I'll need a few hours to arrange things and then I'll come back to you two. You need to rest another day, I think, so I'll stay again tonight. And then we're getting you out of here, Sunny. You will never have to come back to this cellar. Your life will be much different from now on, I promise."

And with that, Sister Ellen sent a silent prayer to God that He would let things work out just as she promised. After all, they needed all the assistance they could get!

Chapter Twenty

Two days later, Sunny and Leah found themselves lying in a warm bed, fresh from the bathtub, wearing new clothes and smelling freshly laundered and pressed sheets.

Just as Sister Ellen had hoped, her friends Eileen and Shirley had come through for them. They had felt an affinity for Sunny over the last couple of months and when Sister came to them to ask for help, they had been happy to. They had an extra bedroom and the means to help the girl out for a while. Besides, they were both looking forward to having a baby around again.

Sunny's carefully collected baby things were transferred in their plastic containers. She was fairly well equipped, but Shirley went shopping to add a crib, changing table, and car seat to her collection.

Eileen took Sister Ellen in her car to go collect Sunny and the baby. Sunny was thrilled that she could stay at *Fat Cat Tales.* She was already familiar with the place and she and Shirley had become fast friends. When she got to the apartment, however, and saw the room that Eileen and Shirley had put together for her, her eyes filled with tears. It was bright and cheerful and perfect.

All of a sudden, Sunny missed her Aunt Gwen. This room reminded her so much of Rancho Manzanillas. Homesickness overcame her in waves and she hugged Leah to her chest, feeling so fortunate that she had a safe place for them both, but feeling incredible grief that such a haven had to come from near strangers and not from her family. They were impossibly far away. Would she ever see them again?

Sunny shrugged off the thought as she realized that Eileen and Shirley and Sister Ellen were waiting for her reaction. They saw her tears as joy and they were joyful in a way. She forced a smile of gratitude to her face to go along with the tears and entered the room and said, "Welcome to your new home, Leah."

Nobody really ever discussed how long Sunny would be allowed to stay with Eileen and Shirley. Their main concern was that she had time to recover from giving birth and that she had plenty of nourishment and warmth while doing it.

Sunny still wanted to try and earn her keep, so she spent part of her days on the blanket outside the door with Leah in her car seat next to her. For some reason, people seemed more interested in the sweet little baby than her artwork, though! She was quickly exhausted by the long feeding-filled nights and the muggy, summer heat, so when Leah signaled that she had endured enough in the seat, then Sunny would pack it up.

Unfortunately, the schedule meant that she wasn't making much money. Shirley and Eileen weren't worried about it, but Sunny wondered how they would ever make it on their own. Sister Ellen was right. She couldn't ever take Leah back to her cellar. It simply wouldn't do for her child to grow up in such a place.

But she couldn't figure out how a sixteen year old, uneducated young mother could get a job that paid enough to cover rent and childcare, not to mention all of the other expenses that occurred when one was on her own.

Shirley and Eileen could see her struggling with her obvious pride and independence. They considered offering her a job at *Fat Cat Tales*, but they simply did not need the help. They were always there and the store required little upkeep. They did offer her small chores, like changing litter and dusting bookcases and emptying garbages, but she refused to take any money from them, as they were already providing food and shelter.

Sunny tried to cool her heels and accept things for what they were, but on a sweltering July day, when Leah was almost three months old, she decided she'd had enough of trying to sell rocks for a mere pittance. She was going to get a real job. She scoured the "Help Wanted" ads for a job close by.

She found resistance from most shop owners, who wanted someone a little older for retail jobs. Besides, she had no nice clothes to wear for that type of work. She didn't have the education she needed for most of the office jobs. So that left food service. There was a pub just down the street that needed a dishwasher for the dinner and evening shift. They would pay her minimum wage, plus a percentage of the bar tips.

Sunny jumped at the chance because it was at a time that *Fat Cat Tales* would be closed and Shirley and Eileen could watch Leah for her. She vowed to save every penny possible so that eventually she and her little girl could be on their own.

Eileen and Shirley were delighted to have more up-close time with Leah Kaye. She was becoming quite charming, full of smiles and coos. Her hair got redder with each passing day and it was clear that her eyes were wide and blue like her mother's. They doted on her incessantly. Sunny swore that they were spoiling her, but she was secretly delighted that they took so much pleasure in watching Leah.

Because she was away from Leah in the evenings, Sunny weaned her slowly and started to feed her daughter infant formula. It was frightfully expensive to feed and diaper a baby! Even with her new wages, she was struggling to buy their necessary clothing and food and diapers and put any of the money away. It was frustrating and Sunny didn't know what she was going to do about it.

Sunny wasn't clear exactly when her feelings began to change about her life with Leah. Perhaps it was when her boss began to demand day shifts too and she had to leave her with Shirley sometimes sixteen hours at a time. She had needed the extra money, so she felt like she had to accept the time when it was offered.

Perhaps her feelings started to change when she observed couples not that much older than herself eating in the restaurant—out on dates, flirting, laughing, and enjoying youth. She longed for the chance to do that. She felt a hundred years old, light years away from ever dating again. It made her sad and jealous and resentful of the hand she had been dealt.

Maybe her feelings changed when Leah was about seven

months old and the holidays were again approaching and she felt enormously homesick, longing for another time when she was at home with her mom and dad and Avery and sneaking open the corners of packages to see if she could tell what they were.

It may have been when Leah finally started reaching for people to pick her up and she instinctively reached for Shirley or Eileen, and rarely for her own mother. It may have been when Leah began to call Shirley 'mama.'

It wasn't that Sunny didn't love Leah with all of her heart. She did—enormously, unconditionally—but she couldn't shake the feeling that she wasn't ever meant to be Leah's mother. She couldn't surmount the feelings of complete inadequacy that overwhelmed her every effort to be a good mother. Sunny couldn't support her daughter financially, emotionally, or physically. She just didn't have the means in any category.

It occurred to her that her daughter would be better off raised by someone other than herself. Young women did give their babies up for adoption. She had never really thought of this as an option while she was pregnant, after all, she had high hopes for her relationship with her child.

But she was learning fast that all of the love in the world couldn't overcome poverty and lack of education.

She pondered the idea of leaving Leah with Eileen and Shirley, but she was pretty sure she could never find the courage to leave her daughter behind as long as their hospitality continued. She decided she would continue to stay the path she was on as long as circumstances allowed.

As it turned out, the decision was taken out of Sunny's hands.

Her figure had come back after she stopped breast-feeding Leah and the owner of the pub, seeing how attractive Sunny was and knowing what a hard worker she had turned out to be, had asked her to be a waitress on the breakfast and lunch shifts. Sunny jumped at the chance because the tips were bigger for waitresses, even if it wasn't the prime time of the day.

So on a crisp February Tuesday, she awoke, showered and dressed in her short black pencil skirt and uniform top and carried Leah in her jammies out to the kitchen. Leah squealed with delight when she saw Eileen reading the paper at the table. Then she pealed with laughter as Shirley popped up from the behind the kitchen counter and yelled, "Boo."

Sunny loved the sound of Leah's laughter and she smiled along as Shirley continued her game of peek-a-boo. The truth was, though, that she was feeling like more and more of an outsider in this home. That feeling stayed with her as she moped her way to work.

She completed the breakfast shift. It appeared to be a slow day, despite the sunshine and clear air. It was just past eleven when Sunny noticed two tall, handsome gentlemen in suits walk in and sit in the window booth nearest the door. They appeared young, but sophisticated and Sunny could smell the expensive cologne surrounding them as she approached the table.

Sunny pulled to a quick stop as the young man with the wavy brown hair and angular face turned his gaze her

170

direction. It was *Avery*! His expression didn't change, so she kept her cool as she approached the table. She did look different than she had a few years ago, more curves, shorter, bobbed hair.

She had lost her scrawny, adolescent look and wisdom had changed her from that stupid kid to a savvy young woman. Would he recognize her?

She needn't have wondered. She was, after all, his only kid sister.

At the words, "What can I get for you," Avery's blue eyes got decidedly rounder with surprise and flew up to meet hers.

"My God in heaven, You must exist. *Sunny?* I can't believe it's you! It *is* you, isn't it?"

"Yes, Avery. It's me. Hi."

"Hi? She says 'Hi.'" To his friend he gestured, "Jonathan, this is my little sister that we have been searching for since over two years ago. And after all that time, she says 'hi.' If you only knew how outspoken she used to be!"

Sunny socked him on the arm for that comment and smiled for the first time since she'd spotted him. She had really missed him, the punk. He jumped up, suit and all, and enveloped her in a giant bear hug. When he finally released her, he held her away from him for a minute.

"You look pretty good, squirt. All grown up."

If only he knew, Sunny thought. But she certainly wasn't going to tell him.

"Well, I'm not a little girl anymore, if that's what you mean."

"I can see that, Sunny. We've been looking for you, you know. We'd almost given up hope because it's been so long."

"I'm sure you mean you and Gwen. Surely Mom and Dad have written me off by now."

"You couldn't be more wrong, Sunny. They've searched just as hard as Gwen and I, calling police stations, the State Patrol, hospitals. You've been listed officially as a missing person since the month that you disappeared. We've missed you, Sunny-girl."

Sunny winced as she heard her father's term of endearment for her. She felt awful that she had caused them all so much worry. She honestly hadn't thought they would care that much.

Sunny's boss approached. She and her young man were causing a scene and there were orders to be taken.

"Sir, I understand your predicament, but this is my long lost little sister that I haven't seen in years. I don't want to cause any trouble, but I am wondering if she could be released from work any earlier today so that we can talk."

Avery's reasonable request was, to Sunny's surprise, met with an equally reasonable reply by the temperamental Irishman, "I'll see if I can call a replacement, Sunny. In the meantime, can you please see about the customers who are waiting?"

Sunny nodded and started with taking Avery and Jonathan's orders. She worked through the next hour until her replacement arrived. Jonathan had needed to return to work—he was an accounting intern at a Madison Avenue firm. Avery had decided to miss the afternoon law class he had back in Tacoma. He sat and drank coffee while he waited for Sunny to finish.

All the while he marveled at the maturity and grace of this new Sunny. She was unflappable, handling orders efficiently, being friendly, yet professional with diners and clearing tables like a champ.

Sunny wondered to herself what she was going to do about Avery. He couldn't have known that her maturity was born from a life of desperation and poverty, that her quiet grace was actually self-confidence, something she had never had during her days in Omak. Sunny knew this about herself: she was an ex-addict, runaway, single, teenage mother. She was also proud, and she was never, ever going to tell her family about any of it. She just couldn't disappoint them that much.

Her hour of work was spent busily doing her job and devising a whopper of a story about where she had been and what she had done during her two years away. She decided that she would take Avery to the Paradise Café after work and feed him the whole story and then they would exchange addresses and then they could get on with their lives, her family none the wiser.

Avery had other plans. He slipped out briefly to use the pay phone at the corner while Sunny was otherwise occupied. He made two calls. One to his advisor at UPS Law School, who needed to know that he would be taking a few days off to take his sister home. The other call was to his parents. He knew Gus would be at work, but there was a chance that Patty would be home for lunch.

The words rushed out as soon as he heard his mother's

voice, "I've found her, Mom."

"Who is this? Avery? Where are you? Who have you found? Surely not…."

"Yes, Mom. It's Sunny. I've found our girl!"

Avery could only hear his mother's sobbing after that. She was obviously trying to regain control, but he stopped her.

"I know, Mom. This is your chance. You don't have to say anything. I'm bringing her home. I'll see you later tonight." He hung up the phone softly. Now he just had to gather up his sister and they would be on their way.

Chapter Twenty-One

The Paradise Café was crowded and Avery didn't see the need to stay there. He wanted to go to Sunny's place so that they could talk in peace. Sunny knew that was out of the question, so she insisted that they take a window seat, since none of the tables were available.

They almost had to shout to hear each other over the crowd. It suited Sunny just fine because she could just stick to small talk. She asked Avery about school and he shared that he was in his final year of law school. He asked her about where she lived, what she'd been doing all of this time. She shared nothing, just glossing over the last two years, saying that she had wanted to live in the big city. She had been tired of boring old Brewster, so one day she just decided to take off, hitchhiking and making her way to Seattle.

No, she didn't know that their grandmother had been hurt. She had left after school that day. She was sorry to hear about it, but admitted that she had been miserable living with the old woman.

Avery didn't buy her story. Sunny forgot that he was in training to ferret out liars in court. She just kept spouting lies and, after a while, Avery just kept listening and finding holes in her story. He had expected Sunny to want to go home. Instead he was sensing that she was trying to get rid of him.

They finished their coffee and Avery asked Sunny if she would go for a walk with him. If they were going to head over the mountains tonight, he needed to do some fast talking to get her to go with him.

They walked down Pine Street and headed South down 12th Avenue toward Seattle University. They walked silently at first and then Avery decided that it was his turn to talk.

"Sunny, I want to tell you first how much I've missed you. I didn't realize how much I cared about you until I couldn't tell you anymore. I had always thought of you as my bratty little sister. It took realizing that I may never see you again for me to admit to myself that you were so much more important than that."

Sunny began to cry softly, "Avery, don't…"

"No, let me tell you more. I can see now that you've had to grow up way too fast. Mom and Dad were wrong to ever kick you out. You're only seventeen and you've been on your own for more than two years. That's just not right.

"What I want you to know is that Mom and Dad even realize how wrong they were."

"They do?" Sunny asked shakily.

"Mom has admitted her mistakes to me many times. She has prayed over and over that she could see you again, so she could just have a second chance to love her only baby girl. Gus hasn't had a drink in I don't know how long."

"*Really*?" Sunny knew how monumental that was for him.

"You should see them, Sunny. They're in love again. It's

like Dad's drinking kept them apart for so long and now they've found each other for the first time. They even play racquetball."

"You're kidding," Sunny giggled a wet giggle. She was actually enjoying this. "How's Aunt Gwen?"

"Not so good, Sunny. Oh, you know Gwendolyn. She's a tough-minded businesswoman. On the surface she's performing as well as she always has. But she was devastated when you left, Sunny. She's been quiet, despondent since then. Truth be told, and I'm not saying this to hurt you, but I think her heart is broken. No one has covered more miles trying to find you than Aunt Gwen."

"I miss her too, Avery, so much. She was more like a mother to me in one year than Mom ever was. I never meant to hurt her."

"I know, Sunny. But you can fix it. You can come home. I'm ready to take you. Tonight."

"But what about Grandma? Will I still be welcome? I can't just go back after all of that, can I?"

"She's in a nursing home, just a raving, bitter old woman. No one cares what she thinks. Why not come back home?"

Sunny could think of many reasons why, Leah being at the top of the list. Her mind was swimming. Every instinct was telling her to go home, but she couldn't do it tonight. She had a daughter to think of and a whole life here.

On the other hand, it still wasn't much of a life. It seemed to her that all she did was work and she still couldn't make ends meet enough to leave the bookstore. She felt further and further away from that initial strong bond she had felt with Leah at first. Sunny was, after all, just a kid. She just wanted to be taken care of, for once, while she was still a child.

"Avery, I want to go home. I really do. But there are a few things that I need to do first. There is someone that I need to visit here at S.U., first of all." She prayed that Sister Ellen would be home. She desperately needed her counsel right now and Sister had become a trusted friend.

Avery was surprised that Sunny had a friend here, but then why wouldn't she? She had been in this neighborhood for a while. He waited in the lobby of Campion Tower while Sunny rode the elevator to the seventh floor.

She headed straight to Sister Ellen's south-facing apartment and held her breath while she knocked on the door.

"Who is it?" Thank God. She was home.

"Sister, it's me, Sunny."

"Why, Sunny," Sister said as she opened the door, "What a nice surprise!" Sunny had only been to her apartment a few times, but Sister Ellen had made it clear that she was always welcome.

"I have a dilemma, Sister, of the hugest proportions."

Sister smiled. She had always been endeared by Sunny's vast vocabulary, so unusual for someone of her limited education. That was the reader in her coming out.

"Well, come on in, then. Let's hear it."

"You'll never guess who's waiting for me downstairs."

"Who?"

"My brother."

"Oh my! Have you told him everything, yet, child?"

Sister was well aware, by now, of Sunny's colorful years away from home. She and the nun were friends and there was nothing that Sunny hadn't shared with this woman.

"No, Sister. I've told him nothing of the sort. And I've decided that I'm not going to. Here's my dilemma—he wants to take me home. And I want to go in the worst way, Sister. My family misses me. Turns out they love me after all and they want a second chance and so do I."

"I understand that, Sunny. You are very young and you deserve to return to your life. Life has been hard for you here."

"That's just it, Sister. It has been hard, but I have never been more proud of myself than when I was on my own, fending for myself, and making it work, no matter how badly I had to scrimp and save."

"You have a sense of accomplishment, as you should. It wasn't easy to do what you did."

"Yes, but now, because of Leah, I am having to accept more handouts. I know that I have to because I don't want my baby to suffer, but I can't help but wonder what kind of a life she's going to have with me. Even if I do eventually make it out on my own, I'll never have the education or means to provide her with the life she deserves."

"That may be true, Sunny, but you will always love her."

"Love's not enough, Sister. I've learned that the hard way—a couple of times."

"What do you want me to say, child? You've come seeking advice. What do you need to hear?"

"I need to hear that you understand why I have to go, Sister. I want you to understand that what I leave behind is going to tear out a piece of my heart. I suppose if you can forgive me when I leave, that God could forgive me too."

"There's nothing to forgive, Sunny. I know that whatever you do will be done out of love, not selfishness. You can go, Sunny. And for what it's worth, I will watch out for your Leah Kaye. I almost feel like her grandmother by now."

Sunny's chest heaved with sobs as she hugged her good friend goodbye for the last time. So it was decided. She had just one more heartwrenching stop to make and then she was going home to stay.

Part Three

Chapter Twenty-Two

"Do you have any idea how lucky you are?"

Leah flipped her long, fire-red mane over her shoulders and shut off her blow-dryer. She turned her wide, blue eyes toward her friend, "What?"

"I said, do you have any idea how lucky you are?" Sharon replied, handing Leah her brush.

"It must be the red hair. It's like a copper penny, heads up. I'm telling you—I have always been lucky."

"Well some of it is deserved, I suppose. After all, you are a brilliant law student with a mind like Einstein and a face and body like a French model."

"Oh, stop! Please. If I looked like a model, do you really think I'd be going to law school with all of these student loans?" Leah rolled her eyes to the heavens, as if He could erase the mountain of debt that went along with private high school, university, and law school educations.

"Well, you are a little short," Sharon deadpanned.

The petite Leah responded with a playful slap to her friend's hand. Sharon was tall and exotic, looking very much like the Brazilian side of her heritage.

"I'm just jealous, Leah. You've got wonderful parents. Look at the place you live—it's hip, cute, and looks out over the funkiest neighborhood in Seattle. You ooze self-confidence. You're gorgeous. And now you're going to intern at Seattle Youth Alliance!"

"Sharon, you really are too much. What about you? You don't have to go to school at all. Your band is debuting at The Autumn Rock Festival this year! You're about to be a megastar. I can't believe you're jealous of *me*! I still live at home, for Pete's sake!"

"I'd live at home too if Broadway was just a stone's throw away! And it's not like your parents are nosey or anything. You have all of the freedom in the world," Sharon replied, then changing the subject, asked, "You really don't know how lucky you are to be going to SeaYA, do you?

Leah pulled her thick mane into a low ponytail and set about applying mascara and a dab of lip gloss.

"I wanted a good internship more than you can imagine. Lord knows I need the money. And I do feel lucky that I got the assignment I wanted. SeaYA has done some wonderful things for young people in the city. And the downtown offices have a gorgeous view of Puget Sound. Mainly, though, I wanted to work with Avery Moss. He was a graduate of SU Law School back when it was owned by University of Puget Sound, so he's an alumnus."

"He's the reason I think you're lucky. Have you *looked* at him?" Sharon fanned herself.

"I should have known that was the reason you were jealous. It had nothing to do with the fact that SeaYA interns have gone on to hugely successful careers in the Seattle law community or that I get to work in civil law thirty hours a week instead of boring tax or real estate law. You just think Mr. Moss is cute."

"Avery Moss is only the most eligible bachelor in the city. He's had everybody from the governor's daughter to the ex-wife of the vice-president of Boeing on his arm. I swear it's that white, white smile and curly brown hair and blue eyes that have bought all of his success."

"He is gorgeous, and brilliant, but way too old for me. I mean, yuck, he could almost be my dad—not that I have one," she quipped.

"Besides, give him credit where it's due. He has said that he decided to found SeaYA because his little sister was a runaway. He wanted young people like her to have a place to turn. He founded SeaYA at a time when Seattle was still flailing its little wings trying to develop social programs. I was just a little kid when he was starting to look out for disadvantaged youth in this community. He's a bona fide role model, not just a hunk."

"You've done your research, haven't you?"

"Of course," Leah replied, "Have you ever known me to be ill-informed?"

"Are you ready yet? I swear it takes you a half-hour just to blow-dry that huge head of hair. The fish market is gonna be sold out of clams by the time we hit the Market."

"You're one to talk," Leah teased her friend, "Just because your hair dries into perfect corkscrew curls doesn't mean you get to make fun of mine. At least I don't need two different colors of eyeliner to complete my look."

"Okay, Miss eau natural, let's get out of here. We've got shopping to do. There won't be many more days of this once September arrives. I'll be so busy plucking my bass guitar and you'll be so busy schmoozing Avery Moss, that we'll never see each other."

"Oh, we'll see each other. After all, you are my bestest friend, Shar. You are right, though. The open air market awaits. Let's hit it."

Leah shouted a quick "Bye, Moms," as she ran out the shop door with her friend into the brilliant Seattle summer day.

Eileen turned to Shirley, looking concerned.

"What's that look for? She certainly looks excited to be getting out. Leah's days of freedom are numbered, you know. Once school starts, she'll be so busy hitting the books and working that she'll never have time to go out. We'll probably never see her," Shirley lamented.

"We never see her now. She lives here, but do we really ever talk to her anymore. We don't even know her friends or if she's interested in any boys in particular. It's probably been a month since we've sat down to one of our chocolate pudding waffle mornings!"

"Don't be worried, Eileen. Most kids her age are living on their own by now. She's twenty-five, for goodness' sake. You and I were already buying our house in San Francisco by the time we were her age."

"I remember. That worries me too. She hasn't had a meaningful relationship yet, either."

"She's been going to school!" Shirley defended. "Besides, she had that one boyfriend, that rocker with the hair down to the middle of his back, when she was an undergrad. Let's just be glad that one didn't last."

Eileen rolled her eyes, "You can say that again!"

They laughed. Eileen looked into her partner's still youthful eyes, and examined her chestnut hair now infused with gray, and her easy smile. Oh, how she loved this woman. And she trusted her completely.

"So you think she's alright? Am I just being a nattering, neglected old mother again?"

"You've always been the conscientious parent, Eileen. You know me. I just love her and hug her and let her make her way. And to think, when we first met, I was the one who was always uptight!

"Yes, Eileen, I think she's okay," Shirley said confidently. "In fact, she's bright, she's beautiful, she's healthy, and she's still *ours*."

Neither one of them could ever forget what a blessing *that* was.

Sister Ellen prepared her morning coffee and sat down to her worktable to continue her latest passion— scrapbooking. She admonished herself silently for sleeping in so long. She could have gotten so much more done had she awoken earlier.

She had always been such an early bird. Somehow, though, unlike most people her age who could hardly sleep at all, she was starting to need more and more rest. She had planned to be up by seven this morning at the very latest and instead had slept until almost ten!

Oh well, she thought, it was a Friday and she really had nowhere to be. She had given up her radio show years ago. That had been a thing of the eighties anyway. Radio had evolved since then—from dream interpretation and synthesized, happy music to political debate shows and angry, loud music. She had no use for it any longer. Although, she thought with a smile, she had heard that some of those eighties bands were making a comeback.

Sister Ellen was still a fixture on campus at the University. She still worked as a receptionist one day a week at Campus Ministry and sat on the advisory board for the Search and Prison Ministry programs. She still had her apartment on the freshman all-girls floor and had a steady stream of young women coming to her for advice and moral support.

As she sat that morning organizing her sixty years worth of sketches, she ran across a sketch of a particularly special young woman. Sister Ellen had never forgotten Sunny. Who *could* forget, after all? In fact she recognized that this sketch was one that she had made only about ten years ago, and it had been at least twenty since she had last seen her.

Or was it more than that? She always had to think how old Leah was to figure that out. Darling Leah was already in her final year of law school, so she guessed that would make her twenty-five. My, how quickly time passed.

Sister studied her drawing of Sunny. It was a sketch she had made from memory after she had dreamed of her once again. Her dreams always featured the young, pregnant Sunny, only they had been framed in sunshine and happy colors since the day Leah had arrived. The scary dreams had vanished once Sister had fulfilled her promise to watch over the girl.

This sketch showed Sunny's wide, clear eyes and full, round face. Of course she had been much thinner by the time she had left Seattle, but this is how Sister most remembered the girl.

It was uncanny how much Leah had grown to look like her mother. All except for that glorious head of red hair— that she must have gotten from the "sperm donor," as she and Eileen and Shirley like to refer to him.

For fun, she scrapbooked the sketch of Sunny on the page opposite of Leah at the age of about six or seven, standing in the door of *Fat Cat Tales*, holding an enormous lollipop that they had gotten earlier that day at Seattle Center. Her eyes were wide with mischief and a sugar high. Sister had sketched this from a photograph Eileen had taken to commemorate a very special day they had all had together.

Sunny would have loved that day, riding the monorail, as Sister was sure she had never done, and eating corn dogs and curly fries for lunch, and viewing the rainy city from the top of the Space Needle.

Leah had been a delight, all full of fun but well-behaved, making intelligent observations about the architecture of the Seattle skyscrapers and amusing them all with the sheer joy she took in having them all together—her special mommies and her Auntie Ellen, as she called Sister.

Sister's eyes misted over as she thought of all the special memories she had of Leah growing up. Leah's mother had missed so much, she could never even imagine. And Sister hadn't even gotten the pleasure of actually living with the child—she had just been a close friend.

Sunny had given them all an immeasurable gift in Leah, but she had made the ultimate sacrifice in doing so. Sister said a quick prayer now, as she often did that Sunny was safe and happy and that her life had become everything she wanted it to be. After all, she had paid the highest possible price.

Chapter Twenty-Three

In fact, Sunny was happy. The day that she had gotten home, she had gone straight into her mom's arms and stayed there for the longest time. Then her dad had joined them. Avery completed the embrace. None of them wanted to let go. And though they had eventually broken their hold, the closeness that came with that reunion had never faded.

Sure, Avery lived in Seattle, but he came home frequently to visit. Sunny never could bring herself to return to Seattle, so she looked forward to his visits to the Okanogan. Her limited adventures led her East or South, never West. Avery didn't quite understand why, but he stayed close to his sister nonetheless, despite her refusal to visit him in his Queen Anne Hill condo. Once he had finished law school, he watched over her from afar.

Sunny had not been allowed to return to high school because she had missed three full academic years, but the alternative high school in Omak had allowed her to get a diploma just a year after her return. She was eighteen by then, with a maturity born of experience her family couldn't possibly understand.

Sunny poured herself into school, wanting to be educated for the sake of living a fruitful life. She was going to be a productive member of society if it killed her.

When she finished her diploma, Sunny enrolled in the local community college. Before they knew it, Gus and Patty Moss were watching the little girl who had once fainted at the sight of blood graduate as a Registered Nurse.

But Sunny didn't stop there. She worked full-time as a nurse for ten years and then earned her master's degree in education from the local branch of University satellite branch. She was currently teaching anatomy and pathophysiology to nursing and radiology students at the community college.

Sunny's parents were endlessly proud of their daughter's accomplishments. She had gone from runaway to student to nurse to educator. She had bought and meticulously restored an old stone house overlooking the town of Okanogan. She had a tabby cat and countless numbers of exotic houseplants. And she painted glorious landscapes and flowers and sunsets, which she displayed in her own enormous house, her relatives houses, and in various venues around town.

Sunny never painted portraits anymore. In the early years after her return home, she sat down several times to work on painting portraits of her loved ones, but each time she did, a little red-headed cherub would invade her thoughts. How she longed to paint that face just so that she could see it again! But she would dismiss the thoughts and paint something else. She couldn't afford to think about Leah—her heart was still too fragile even after all of these years.

In fact, as close as Sunny was to her mom and dad and Avery and her Aunt Gwen, whom she visited often at

Rancho Manzanillas, she had never let anybody else even close enough to love her. She was still a bit of a loner, preferring a warm fire and a good book to an evening out with acquaintances. Portia, the tabby cat, was easily her best friend.

Now nearly forty-two years old, Sunny had never seriously dated anyone since returning home, nor had she cultivated any close friendships. Friends and boyfriends had gotten her into immeasurable amounts of trouble when she was a teen. She had no need for them now. She had a career, a home, several fulfilling hobbies, and a supportive family.

Life was good. Okay, so maybe she had hidden the biggest event of her life—her daughter's birth—from the people who now loved her the most. So she had left out her drug addiction and illegal activities from the story she had told them all about her time away. And perhaps she was just the slightest bit bereft, missing that part of herself that used to feel angry, love deeply, and express emotion freely.

Sunny Moss had spent most of her adult life trampling down the free spirit that had defined her teenage years. She was an unnaturally controlled person during times of stress, as many coworkers could attest from working with her as a nurse. They admired her calm demeanor and sharp intelligence, but they admired her from a distance.

Sunny was now a model of the community. If only they knew her secrets. Nobody in her family would have ever guessed how much she struggled with herself over the decisions she had made, the relationships she had left behind. What really mattered was that she herself would never escape them.

She had spent twenty-five long years denying herself the emotions that accompanied those decisions. But she had a lot to be proud of too and that is where she focused her thoughts one day at a time.

It was late August when Avery came home for his customary summer break. He took two weeks off every summer so that he could waterski, fish, hunt birds, attend rodeos, play tennis; whatever struck his fancy.

Sunny thought it was funny how he always came home for that two weeks. He was a wealthy lawyer. He could have gone anywhere to enjoy his favorite activities. But he always came home. He always said that his favorite fishing hole, the city slough in Okanogan, would feel neglected were he not to visit at least once or twice a year.

In truth, Avery enjoyed his family now more than ever. He was still single, looking for just the right woman to fit into his very busy life, and he couldn't think of anyone he'd rather be around for the summer break than his mom, his step-dad, and his sister.

This year was a little different, though. He was bringing a friend of his home with him. Dennis Fulton was the chief financial officer at Seattle Youth Alliance. Avery had founded the organization, but Dennis had not been far behind in joining the team. They had known each other for at least twenty years.

Dennis had never been to the Okanogan with Avery, however, and until just a few years ago, his wife and kids had kept him too busy to take a summer break anywhere.

His kids were in college now, though, and his wife, Shelby, had died tragically just two years before when she was thrown from a horse headlong into a fence post.

Avery had noticed that Dennis was working unusually long hours and that he was compelled to stop and talk with Avery more often than before. He would jump at any chance that Avery would offer to occupy his time after work hours. It was simple to figure out—the guy was lonely and he missed his wife terribly.

When Avery had mentioned his yearly break, Dennis had hinted that he would like to see the Okanogan Valley sometime. He had heard about the Eastern Washington playground from some of his hunting buddies. And he'd always wanted to see the World Famous Suicide Race, a daring downhill horse race that made Omak Stampede Rodeo so popular.

Avery had felt compelled to ask his old friend along. After all, he felt sorry for the guy and Dennis was really good company, aside from his occasional brooding over being a widower. He liked the outdoors and he had an infectious sense of humor, accompanied by a booming laugh. It might be fun to hang out during the summer with another guy.

Patty was a nervous wreck getting ready for an unknown guest, especially someone as accomplished as Avery claimed Dennis was. She worried that her house wasn't fancy enough or that her old guest room with its lavender walls and ivy décor wouldn't be suitable for a big-city accountant.

She needn't have worried. Dennis was laid back and

ready for a vacation. He would have slept in their camp trailer if he'd had to. Besides, his wife had been an interior decorator—there wasn't a flower or wallpaper or paint color he hadn't been made to endure during their twenty-eight year marriage.

In just a few days' time, it was as if Dennis had always been there. He and Gus hit it off quickly, talking about guy things—guns, hunting, fishing, racquet sports. Avery might have been jealous of the quick bond Dennis and Gus formed, but he was too occupied by his doting mother to really have time to notice.

Sunny noticed, though. She had worried over whether she would get any time alone with her brother while he was home, since he wasn't by himself this time. It was summer quarter and she was teaching just one class, so she was bored herself and had looked forward to Avery's break to keep occupied.

Sunny attended dinner the first night of their stay, dreading the influence an outsider might have on her brother's demeanor, especially since it was someone he worked with. As it turned out, she quite enjoyed herself. Dennis had grown up in Southern California and he regaled them with funny stories about fake blonds and swimming pools in every yard and oodles of people everywhere you went.

Dennis had a commanding presence. He was as tall as Avery, but much broader through the shoulders and slightly thick through the waist. He had sandy blond hair and eyes the color of melted chocolate. Sunny thought he looked every inch like someone's husband. She was rather

194

surprised to hear that he was not married.

Sunny had never heard a laugh quite like Dennis' before. It rumbled up from his toes and came out in a deep timber, reverberating off the walls of her mom's small dining room. His humor was absolutely contagious and she found herself smiling, despite herself and her own preoccupations.

At the end of the night, Dennis took her aside, "It was so nice to meet you, Sunny. I understand that you were Avery's whole inspiration for SeaYA. I can see why your family missed and needed you so much. You fit here. You are all such wonderful people."

"That's kind of you to say. There have been rougher times in the Moss family, but that is ancient history. I'm glad to be here too. I'm especially proud of Avery for all that he's done for kids and the city of Seattle. If I had any small part in inspiring him, then I have people like you to thank for making SeaYA such a success."

"From what he tells me, you've made quite a success of yourself also," Dennis replied.

Sunny shied away from the flattery. "Just how much has Avery shared about me?"

"Just that you're a teacher at the college and an accomplished nurse and that you own one of the biggest, oldest houses in Okanogan."

'And that I'm a spinster, in need of a husband,' Sunny thought to herself. Is that what Avery was up to? She was suspicious, automatically, of single men trying to flatter her. Was her brother trying to match-make?

"You know, Sunny, I don't usually talk this much. My wife Shelby was always the outgoing one. She hardly let any of us get a word in edgewise!"

Sunny was surprised to hear him talk about his wife. Was he divorced, then?

"Shelby died a few years ago in a horseback riding accident. It seems like I've spent all that time trying to fill in the silences left by her absence."

Sunny suddenly felt like an ass. Suspicion over why this man was talking to her turned into sorrow for him and his family.

"Do you have children?" She found herself more curious than ever about this man.

"Three, actually. Our twin girls, Cadence and Felicia are at USC. They spent the summer there working on a dormitory painting crew and living with my baby sister. Our youngest, Jacob, will be a sophomore at Columbia University, studying architecture. He had to stay for a preceptorship this summer."

"They're so far away!" No wonder he talked so much, Sunny thought, he's got to be terribly lonely. She certainly knew how that was, but then she'd had lots of time to get used to being alone. She made a resolution right there and then to be kind to this man on his stay in the Okanogan. It couldn't hurt for him to have another friend. For that matter, it couldn't hurt for her to have a friend either. Could it?

Chapter Twenty-Four

The Okanogan Valley had changed considerably since Sunny and Avery's childhoods. There were still the same basic old buildings lining the downtown areas of Omak and Okanogan, but the mom-and-pop businesses had been replaced by specialty shops and boutiques aimed at surviving the competition leveled by the super store up the highway.

There were a handful of fast-food chain restaurants, but these hadn't entirely taken the place of the few charming eateries that managed to survive. Originality was required in order to thrive as the towns seldom visited by outsiders came to rely on tourism dollars. The combination of good restaurants and fun shops with outlying lakes and rivers and game land that remained relatively unspoiled made the depressed county more of a destination as the years passed.

There were far more strangers than Sunny had ever known of in her childhood. She was ambivalent about the changes because they meant a better overall economy, but she did miss the innocence of the County back in the days when it had only one stoplight.

Dennis was delighted with it all. As far as he was concerned, Okanogan County was the best-kept secret of summer fun and recreation that Washington State had. He and Avery fished at the slough in Okanogan and at all three of the lakes in the Conconully area. They hunted pheasant up the Chiliwist. They waterskied at Omak Lake, a pristine alkali lake on the Colville Indian Reservation. They attended the Tonasket Founder's Day and Omak Stampede rodeos.

And in the evenings, he got to see Sunny. He found himself looking forward more and more to the balmy summer nights when they hung up their fishing poles and visited with Avery's remarkably warm family. He liked them all a great deal. But he especially liked Sunny.

Sunny had a wonderful time with her brother during his two-week stay. Her growing friendship with Dennis was just an added bonus. She hosted the two of them several times at her home. It was all very fun and very safe. As long as Avery was along, she needn't worry about Dennis getting the wrong idea.

But Sunny was starting to get the wrong idea herself. She was *attracted* to him. Her mom had noticed Sunny's fascination with Dennis and like all moms with single, eligible daughters, she was cultivating ways for Dennis and Sunny to be alone. She even tried, unsuccessfully, to occupy Avery during times when Sunny might be trying to spend time with both of them.

Sunny resolved that she would not fall for Dennis, despite his contagious laughter and soulful brown eyes. She would be his friend. That was all. She had been in love once and look where it had taken her. She would never pay a price like that again.

It was on their final night in Omak that Patty hosted Aunt Gwen and Sunny, as well as Avery and Dennis. Gwendolyn noticed Dennis and Sunny's chemistry right away. She was happy for her niece, but she could see that Sunny was still fighting it.

Gwendolyn never pried where Sunny was concerned, but she somehow knew that Sunny's time away had been traumatic for the girl. One doesn't change that much without serious life challenges. She never understood fully why Sunny didn't seek companionship for herself, but she of all people could comprehend being content with solitude. After all, she had never remarried after Alberto. Her life and Sunny's weren't all that different, but at least Gwendolyn had known happiness with a man, if only too briefly.

Gwendolyn followed Sunny to the powder room after dessert to present her case. As Sunny was emerging, she simply said, "He likes you, you know."

Sunny was taken aback, "Who are you talking about?"

"You know who. Dennis. The big teddy bear with the chocolate eyes. I'm not sure what made me want to stroke him more, that fuzzy head of thick sandy hair or the soft green wool sweater he was wearing!"

"Aunt Gwen! You're at least fifteen years older than Dennis."

"How old is he, dear?"

"I'm not sure. I haven't asked him that. I do know that he was married for twenty-eight years and that he has grown children. He must at least be in his fifties. He doesn't look that old, though, does he?"

"Hmmm, you've given this some thought, I see. Well, age is relative, Sunny. After all, I don't look a day over fifty myself," Gwendolyn grinned a youthful smile.

"I like him too, Aunt Gwen," Sunny was solemn as she said it.

"Then what *is* the problem?"

"It seems silly to fall in love now when I've so settled on being a spinster!" Sunny laughed a bitter laugh.

"Seriously, Sunny. You need to do what makes you happy. If you could really care about this man, you shouldn't let anything hold you back. I've always sensed, since your return, that you've withdrawn. That spark you had when you left has flickered out.

You know that I have never demanded to know why. That's not our style, now is it?"

Sunny shook her head.

"But whatever happened to you, however it happened, that was almost twenty-five years ago, for goodness' sake. I've always loved to give you advice and here's my latest: Go for it, girl. He's a peach. And I'm ready to see you fall madly in love for once."

Sunny's eyes filled with tears. She always did love her Aunt Gwen. She hugged her and told her she'd think about what she said.

Dennis was carrying a big torch for Sunny by that night and he knew that he had to let her know before he and Avery left town. He was struggling with his feelings, though. Guilt bubbled to the surface every time he thought about moving on.

200

Shelby had been his whole life. She had been vivacious and smart and every inch as in love with him as he had been with her. They had only been eighteen when they met their freshman year of college. They had married as soon as they graduated.

They were supposed to be partners forever. Then she died. How could he ever really love someone else?

He wasn't sure how much he cared for Sunny. He just knew that he had felt that undercurrent of attraction. He could tell she felt that way too.

He liked the way her gorgeous wide blue eyes lit up when she laughed. She had to be at least forty, but she still had a trim build, with curves in all the right places.

He admired her obviously strong work ethic, both in how she'd restored her beautiful old house and in her art and career. She was educated far beyond most of the people who grew up and worked here. It was remarkable given the rough start she'd had as a teenage runaway. He was completely stymied as to why she'd never married.

Avery had sensed earlier that week that something was going on with his old friend and his sister. If he felt anything, it was relief that she was finally letting someone past that careful barrier she had erected since returning home. Dennis was a good man—stable, dependable, and fun-loving. He couldn't think of a better guy to hook his little sister up with.

When the three of them ended up on the back deck, catching the cool night air and enjoying one last beer, Avery took his cue to leave the two of them alone.

Dennis fidgeted for a few minutes, peeling the label off

his beer and shifting his body weight from one foot to the other. He cleared his throat.

"Sunny, I've been meaning to ask you something."

"What is it?"

"Well, you see, I don't normally ask women out. I mean, I haven't dated since Shelby died and I met her when I was eighteen, so I never got much of a chance before then, anyway…."

"Out with it, Dennis! Are you going to ask me out? Is that what this is?" Sunny smiled with delight, as she teased him.

"Don't torture me, Sunny. Can't you see me sweating?" He laughed back at her. "Seriously, though, I want you to come see me in Seattle. I think you're a really special lady and I want to get to know you better."

"I can't, Dennis."

"Can't what? Can't go out with me? Can't get to know me better? What?"

"I can't go to Seattle, Dennis. Hasn't Avery told you? I've never been back there."

"Well no wonder I haven't met you before. Can you tell me why?"

"The truth is, I'm not quite sure why. I think it's just bad memories of too many struggles, too much pain," she lied.

"I'm going to try and change your mind, Sunny. I really want to see you again. In the meantime, we can write letters and emails and I'll call you, but I'm staying in touch. I'm not going to let the simple matter of geography stand in our way."

"I'll be happy to correspond with you, Dennis. I think

you're a remarkable man. And you're friends with my brother—he has impeccable taste, you know."

"He reminds me all of the time. Seriously, though, I must see you again."

"Don't worry, Dennis. You'll be seeing me. That's a promise."

They smiled again at each other, each tingling with the feeling of newfound infatuation. Dennis leaned toward Sunny and gave her the softest, most powerful kiss she had ever felt. They ignored the nightfall as they reveled in that kiss, holding each other quietly, each wondering where this was going to lead.

Avery called his parents and Sunny as soon as he got home. It was tradition in their family to call as soon as one landed so that everyone else could rest easy that their loved one was safe.

Sunny no sooner hung up with Avery and her phone rang again. It was Dennis.

"I miss you already," he lamented.

"I miss you too, both of you. Don't you wish sometimes that you could simply blink and be where you wanted to be, no matter how far away?"

"It's only about four and a half hours, Sunny, close enough to drive over on a long weekend. Don't forget that, okay?"

"Okay, Dennis," she sighed. How could he possibly understand that to her Seattle might as well be the North Pole—unreachable? "I'll talk to you soon," she murmured, feeling as sad as the dead line sounded as she rang off.

Chapter Twenty-five

Leah was a nervous wreck as she got dressed for her first day at Seattle Youth Alliance. She had picked out a teal green suit with a gray shell, an outfit that showed off her blaze of red hair. By that Monday, though, the outfit seemed too bold, almost garish. She wanted to make the best possible impression.

She put on the outfit, took it off, then tried khaki slacks and a navy blazer. She looked in the mirror. Yikes. She looked like she was wearing her high school uniform! She shrugged off that outfit and piled it on top of the other. Her mom was going to kill her for not taking better care of her clothes, but she hadn't expected to have a clothing crisis. She was running out of time!

Finally, after rifling through her closet yet again, she pulled out a fitted pants suit she'd had a few years. It was black with white pinstripes and coupled with her three-inch heels, it made her petite frame look very slim, but much taller than it actually was. She put the gray shell with it and pulled her thick hair into a quick French braid. As always, she wore minimal make-up.

She bounded down the stairs, shiny-eyed and fresh looking, but very much in a hurry. She had five minutes to hit the bus stop two blocks away or she would be late.

Talk about making a good impression—being late would definitely botch that.

She gave her moms quick kisses on the cheeks and they handed her a canvas lunch bag with a thermos of today's soup of the day and an organic breakfast bar. She smiled her thanks and raced out the door.

Leah made her bus and got downtown with about ten minutes to spare. Breathing a quick sigh of relief, she walked the remaining block to SeaYA and glided through the front doors. The Seattle Youth Alliance was in an old five-story brick building at the edge of Pioneer Square.

The first level was obviously geared toward the young clients that SeaYA served. It was a completely open space with a reception counter surrounded by colorful groups of overstuffed chairs and acrylic coffee tables. Between the seating groups were pinball machines, pool, foosball, and air hockey tables, and old-fashioned video arcade games.

The music overhead was top-forties and the receptionists were dressed very casually in baggy jeans and tie-dyed t-shirts displaying various SeaYA logos. The girl that greeted Leah couldn't have been more than twenty. She had lovely chocolate brown hair infused with strips of royal purple. Everything about her was hip, from her funky hair to her chunky-rimmed glasses to her polka-dot sneakers.

Leah suddenly felt very conservative. She hoped that the other legal department interns were dressed more like she was. The girl was friendly as she created a photo ID for Leah and directed her to the fourth floor, Human Resources, where she would go through orientation.

This was to be a full eight-hour day being orientated

and greeted by the legal staff. After today she would be working just five hours on either end of her already full class schedule. Leah was practically humming with nerves by the time she reached HR. She was excited, but anxious to get on with it.

There were just four other interns and apparently, though she was on time, she was the last to arrive. She was happy to see them dressed conservatively also. Two of the others, like herself, were law students from S.U. The other two were from the University of Washington MBA program. The five of them, three men and two women, would work at SeaYA over the course of the nine-month academic year, though they would work in very different capacities.

Leah was her usual outgoing self, being friendly to these people, though she knew that she would see little of them once they reached their different departments. She had been assigned to the *pro bono* section of the legal department. Her counterparts were in the *guardian ad litum* and family law sections. The MBA students were to work exclusively in the finance department under the Chief Financial Officer, Dennis Fulton.

To her surprise the first part of their orientation was a personal greeting from Avery Moss himself. He was every bit as handsome in person as he had appeared on television and in the news. Actually, he was much more engaging than she had expected. He seemed genuinely interested in teaching them all the value of helping the youth of the community live better lives and get the help they needed to achieve that.

After giving a short pep talk, Avery spent a short time

talking to each one of them about their assignments. He encouraged them to direct any pressing questions to their immediate supervisors, but made it clear that his door would always be open should they need advice or mentoring.

When Avery met Leah, he couldn't shake the feeling that there was something uncannily familiar about her. He would have to check later and see if they'd had a brother or a sister of hers work for them previously.

In the meantime, he informed Leah that *pro bono* was near and dear to him because the free legal services provided by them were the only kind that SeaYA had offered at first. He had basically graduated from law school and made himself into a free lawyer for kids who needed emancipation from their parents or help navigating the social services offered to homeless, underage kids or to young mothers trying to get financial support from the fathers of their children.

Avery had lived in a dump of an apartment in China Town and eaten Top Ramen for almost every meal while he helped as many kids as he could from his tiny Pioneer Square office. It was only a few years before he had gathered government and private funding to expand SeaYA into the organization it was today, moving it to a larger building and offering services to still more homeless and lost and troubled kids.

Most services were still offered with little or no cost to the clients they served, so arguably, the whole legal department could be known as *pro bono.* There were things they did now, though, like guardian ad litem that were funded by local social service agencies and the State of Washington.

Leah was directed to her supervisor, Lenny Morales, to complete her orientation and to meet the rest of her department. Mr. Moss moved on to the next intern and Leah, feeling honored to work with such a humble and obviously emotionally invested leader, looked forward to contributing to this wonderful organization. She was going to show her mettle as a legal intern. And she was going to give her all trying to impress Avery Moss.

Dennis Fulton finished doing his part of the MBA orientation shortly before eleven. He was looking forward to his lunch date. He'd had a standing date every third Monday for the last thirty years and time had not dulled the pleasure he felt at each of these meetings.

Dennis had loved four women in his life. His mother was the first, but she had died while he was a senior in college. His wife had filled the void she left behind, giving him his three delightful children and nurturing him every bit as much as his mother had. Of course he had to love his little sister. The fourth love of his life was Sister Ellen Ryan.

Before his days at Seattle Youth Alliance, Dennis' first job had been at a small Seattle radio station, acting as the accountant and payroll clerk and human resources director, all while finishing his master's degree. Sister Ellen had been on his payroll and it was then that she had stolen part of his very young heart.

Sister was twenty years his senior and he'd developed

a sort of reverence for her. First of all, she was the most deeply spiritual person he had ever known. Early on, she had been the reason he sought faith in the first place. His parents had really never taken him to church. He had no religious background or training. Sister had led him to the Church and he and his family would be forever grateful for the guidance it gave them.

Later, when he lost Shelby, Sister Ellen was the only reason he didn't lose faith altogether. His children were away and immersed in grief themselves. He had very few lifelines to lead him through his darkest time. Sister had understood and provided her own brand of quiet support and prayer.

Sister Ellen also kept him grounded. She had always teased him mercilessly about his "puppy-dog eyes," telling him it was only her complete devotion to her vocation that kept her from "jumping his bones." She had taken a very young, very serious accountant and taught him how to laugh and poke fun at our quirky world.

In truth, he'd always been a little shocked at her defiance of convention. Most nuns he knew didn't read palms or interpret dreams or carry a pack of Tarot cards in her purse. But then, that was why he loved her. She was unique, a devoted friend and an unwavering spiritual mentor.

Dennis called to check in on Sister Ellen frequently. And then there was their once a month standing lunch date. They always met at Pizzaro's Pizza because Sister insisted on a once monthly helping of cheese-laden, delicious, floppy, Chicago-style pizza. She knew Dennis could match her slice for slice, so he was the only lunch partner sure to finish a whole pizza with her. Leftovers from a Monday lunch date were unheard of.

He passed by the triangular 15th and Madison building, looking for parking that day and saw Sister pulling open the door. She had likely walked the distance from campus. She had been traipsing all over this Hill since he had been in nursery school. She had never, to his knowledge, driven herself anywhere.

He parked his car two blocks away and walked back to Pizzaro's. Perhaps Sister Ellen had it right. Parking was such a hassle—why drive? (Though he really couldn't imagine leaving Shelby's sweet, yellow Beetle at home every day. His hulking body loved the contrast of the zippy little car—he had taken to driving it every day from his West Seattle home to the city.)

Dennis was all smiles as he opened the door and saw Sister sitting at their regular booth, waiting patiently for his arrival. She looked ethereal as ever in a gauzy, rainbow-colored caftan, but Dennis could see from a distance that she looked tired around the edges. That was definitely unusual.

He was almost to the table before she broke her reverie. "Oh, Dennis, dear. I didn't even see you come in!"

"Hiya Sweetheart," he gave her the usual greeting and a fat kiss on each of her deeply wrinkled cheeks.

This made her smile, as it always did. She replied, "Darling. You mustn't. People will talk, you know," and then she winked and squeezed his ample cheeks.

He winked back at her and sat opposite her in the booth. The waitress already knew what their order would be so after a quick greeting, she set their lunch in motion.

Sister wasted no time getting to what was on her mind.

"So tell me about this young woman that you met just before our last luncheon, Dennis. Have you spoken with her?"

"You never beat around the bush, do you, Sister Ellen? I was going to start with a 'how are you doing?' and a question about your residents, you know, small talk."

"You know me, dear, I can't be bothered with insignificant chatter. I like the nitty-gritty and since your love life has always been far more interesting than mine, I must know if there is any news in that department."

"I might as well tell you, since you're going to drag it out of me anyway. I'm not sure if anything is going to develop with my young woman or not. We have written emails and talked on the phone. If anything, I'm even more interested than I was when I met her. She's so intelligent and articulate and confident. But in a way, she seems vulnerable too."

"That ought to appeal to you. You are a natural knight in shining armor. Why do you sound uncertain about this now? Last month you seemed thrilled and excited about a possible future with this girl. You were positively giddy!"

"She won't come here. To Seattle, I mean. I've asked her over for the weekend several times. She's a teacher and her academic year is just starting. I was hoping she would visit before then. She won't even consider it."

"Well, maybe she's traditional. It's not exactly proper to stay at a man's house when you've only just met him."

Dennis blushed. "Sister Ellen! I wasn't going to make

her sleep with me. Just stay at my house or with Avery for that matter. I just wanted to show her around town."

"Oh, of course, dear. I didn't mean to embarrass you." Sister smiled at Dennis' obvious discomfort talking with her about dating. It was very new to him, after all, having been married all of those years.

"Why do you suppose she won't come to Seattle, Dennis? Didn't you say that her brother lives here also?"

"She's very evasive about that. I've asked Avery, but he has no clue either. He's done plenty of talking over the years trying to get her to visit, but she refuses. He thinks it has to do with her time here as a runaway. Post-traumatic stress or something."

"Oh, how interesting. I had forgotten that Avery Moss founded your company because of her. I had quite missed that connection. She was homeless here in Seattle?"

"I guess so. They lost her when she was fourteen and she disappeared for a couple of years. They found her just when they had given up hope. According to Avery she was in perfectly good health, looking well anyway, when he found her, so he didn't suspect abuse or ill treatment. But she's been unwilling to ever share her story completely and he's suspects the trauma goes deeper than she will ever disclose."

"How sad for her that she hasn't found someone to tell the whole story to."

"I think so. I'm sort of hoping that someday she'll be willing to share it with me."

"So you care about her, Dennis? It sounds like you do."

"I could, Sister Ellen, a great deal. But I lost my soul

mate in Shelby. I don't know how to do love halfway. She's going to have to trust me enough to come here someday."

"Give her time. But it sounds like you shouldn't let her go because of simple geography."

"That's what I said originally too."

"Tell me about her." The pizza arrived and Sister started munching as Dennis shared his love's interests.

"….And, Sister, she is the most incredible artist. I've never seen quite so many colors in a painting of a sunset before. But those kind of sunsets are real in Eastern Washington. I got to see one while I was there…."

"She paints, you say?" Sister was always interested in other artists.

"Oh, yes. And she doesn't just paint landscapes or sunsets. And she doesn't apparently always use canvas. She has these great big flat stones in her entryway that have sunflowers and kale on them that look life-like enough to touch."

Sister's eyes glazed over as her mind started to put together pieces from a puzzle begun long ago.

"Kale, huh? I have some smaller stones myself with kale paintings on them. Not everyone can get the colors of those plants just right."

"She did. It's amazing. She's very talented."

"I'm not sure if I've ever asked you, Dennis. It seems such a minor detail, but you've never told me this young woman's name."

"Oh yeah. I didn't mean for her to just be the mystery woman," Dennis rolled his eyes as he wolfed down half a slice of pizza in one generous bite. He finished chewing.

"Her name really fits her personality, Sister Ellen. It's Sunny. Sunny Moss."

Sister could have been a master poker player as she tried very hard to hide the shock she was feeling inside. This was bigger than a coincidence.

God had brought her friend Sunny back to her.

Chapter Twenty-six

Sister Ellen had a heart attack late that evening.

She was washing her dinner dishes, mulling over her earlier conversation with Dennis, when the most horrible pain she had ever felt shot from the middle of her chest down her left arm.

She grabbed her arm and leaned forward against the sink. She gasped as the running water soaked the front of her blouse. She stepped away from the sink and leaned against the counter behind her, trying to mop up the water, but still feeling the terrible ache in her left chest.

She tried to catch her breath, but a deep breath seemed to be beyond her reach. When the second stabbing pain shot clear down to her fingers, she fell to the floor. Recognizing that she was in trouble, Sister decided to crawl to the phone, rather than to risk falling again.

She dragged herself to the phone stand. The first person she could think to call was Father Milton, the priest who moderated the all-boys floor above her and acted as her counterpart. He would know what to do and since she was most certainly dying, she might need him to administer her last rites.

Father Milton had the paramedics at the residence hall within minutes. He rushed to Sister Ellen's aid and tried to keep her calm while they waited for help to arrive.

It was all a blur after that. Sister remembered vaguely being sedated and taken for an angiogram. She was in recovery when the cardiologist came to see her and murmured something about 'unable to stent' and 'occluded' and 'irreparable damage.' It was all so vague and happening so quickly.

Father Milton and Sister's good friend and coworker, Judy Savadge, from Campus Ministry stayed by her side throughout the night.

By morning, Sister Ellen's sedation was completely gone. Drugs were keeping any pain she had at bay. Father Milton and Judy were talking quietly in the hall outside her door. They looked mournful as they came inside and noticed that she was awake.

"You two look like you lost a best friend. I'm still here, aren't I? I had a heart attack, didn't I?"

"You sure gave us a scare," Judy replied.

"And yes, Ellen, you are still here, by some sort of miracle," responded Father Milton.

"God must still have work for me to do," Sister shrugged and smiled.

"Do you remember what the doctors told you last night, Sister Ellen?" Judy asked.

"I really don't recall much from last night. Do you think you could get them to fill me in again this morning? After I take another nap, that is?"

"Of course, Ellen. You rest. We will make sure Dr. Schultz, your cardiologist, comes to see you today," Father Milton offered.

"I'll just rest for a while, then. Thank you both. Perhaps you can go home and get some rest now as well."

Her two friends took her at her word and went home to rest. They planned to return in the early afternoon, but Dr. Schultz arrived before they did. He was a busy man and, once he reviewed Sister Ellen Ryan's chart once again, he braced himself to give her the news.

"Good, you're awake. How do you feel today, Sister Ellen?"

"I'm exhausted. It seems like every time I open my eyes a giant lead weight pulls them shut again. You must be Dr. Schultz. My friends said that you would stop by."

"Would you rather have them here while we talk?"

"Oh dear, no. I'm not worried about that. By their expressions and my vague memories of last night, I'm with the understanding that your news is not good.

What you need to know about me, Dr. Schultz, is that I am every inch a woman of faith. You just tell me the truth and God will handle the rest. There is nothing you can say that will frighten or alarm or devastate me. Go ahead, then. I can take it, Doctor."

"You survived a major heart attack last night. It is actually remarkable that you survived it and you're not out of the woods just yet. We, your other doctors and I, feel like with rest and cardiac rehab, you will go home again."

"Keep going, Doctor."

"But, your heart muscle has been devastated by the damage that was done. You have two major arteries that are completely occluded. Once they get to that point, they cannot be stented, which we had hoped to do during your catheterization.

The next logical step for someone in your situation is open-heart surgery. We can bypass the occlusions with veins from the leg and restore blood flow to the rest of the heart. Normally, however, we try to do this while the heart muscle is as strong as possible. Your heart, Sister Ellen, is very weak. The possibility is huge that you would not survive such a surgery."

"That is if I was willing to have you crack open my chest, is that it?"

"It is an option, Sister Ellen. Your choices are just very limited. I'm sorry."

"So I could elect for a surgery that will likely kill me or I could go on with my weary heart the way it is?"

"That's pretty much it, yes."

"Just how long do I have should I let things alone?"

"We can give you medications to fend off chest pain and keep the rest of your circulation going for now. But your heart will have to eventually give up. As you said, it is definitely weary.

It is so hard to predict these things. We as doctors are asked very often to give people time lines, percentages for survival. What we can never account for is the strength or weakness of the person receiving that news. You, I suspect, Sister Ellen, are very strong. I'm guessing that you will survive just as long as you really want to, won't you?"

"Dr. Schultz, you flatter me. What we both know, though, is that this particular situation is beyond our control."

"If I had to guess, I would give you six months at the outset."

"Six months. I think I can have things in order by then. I won't be having any surgeries, Dr. Schultz. I've lived a full, satisfying life and my God is waiting for me. I don't want any extreme measures to prolong things, or shorten them, as it may be," Sister Ellen looked down at her bed and smoothed her sheets. Then she looked back up at Dr. Schultz.

"Thank you for your candor, Doctor. You just let me know when I can return home. Beyond that, your job is done."

"I'll make you as comfortable as I can for however long you are with us, Sister Ellen. You just let the nurses know if you need anything at all."

"I will."

As he quietly left the room, Sister considered crying. Six months was an awfully short time to spend with all of the people she knew and loved. She thought about mourning her own mortality. But that only lasted a few minutes.

It only lasted as long as it took for her to remember that she only had a few more months before she got to meet the angels and fold herself into the arms of her Savior. She had been looking forward to *that* adventure for nearly seventy years!

There were just few things left to put in order before that happened.

Chapter Twenty-seven

Sister Ellen Ryan was dying, slowly, but surely. She made sure that fact was shared with only a few people. She returned home with a full-time nurse. She welcomed visitors as always, but her weak heart kept her from going out as she used to.

She spent much of her time organizing her scrapbooks and putting her papers in order and figuring out what to do with the earthly possessions she would leave behind.

By Christmas, Dennis Fulton noticed her absence rather acutely. She had let him know that their standing lunch date would have to be postponed until further notice. She was ill, that he knew from visiting her at home, but she assured him that her situation was just temporary (neglecting to tell him that it was also terminal.)

Leah, Shirley, and Eileen all came to visit as well while Leah was enjoying her final Christmas break. They knew their friend was quite ill and had been for several months, but she gave them no reason to fear any finality about their visit. They simply brought her some books and wished her a speedy recovery and chatted with her merrily as they always did.

They all went on with their lives, as she waited patiently for hers to end.

Dennis decided to take a trip to Eastern Washington. He just had to see Sunny again, in person. They had continued to correspond. He had always been skeptical of long-distance or Internet romances. How could they possibly be expected to last when the physical limitations existed so prominently?

He was learning just exactly how that was possible. He had shared things via email and the telephone that he may never have gotten to talk about in person. For one thing, when you're actually with a person, you spend quiet time, watching movies, eating, making love. There are a lot of silences. But when you are away from each other, all of the time on the phone or on the computer or writing letters is spent communicating. Sunny probably knew as much about him as Shelby had. In four short months he had fallen hard for Sunny Moss. He had to see her again to see if she felt the same way.

Sunny did. She was in love and terrified. Dennis was everything she'd ever dreamed of in a mate. He was smart and witty and warm and wise. He wrote eloquently and she just loved the deep timber of his voice over the phone as he lay in bed talking to her late into the night, both of them too exhausted to stay awake, but so unwilling to say goodnight from afar.

Dennis had become a romantic voice in the night, a sweet note on the computer first thing in the morning, and a lovely bunch of flowers on her birthday, and on Halloween, and on Thanksgiving, or any other event he could think of to send flowers for. In fact she had quite forgotten how

Dennis looked and tasted and felt, but she was looking forward to being reminded.

It was just so easy to love Dennis. However, Sunny knew she was going to have to reconcile with her past to carry this relationship further. In a way Sunny was relieved because she'd been so lonely living with her memories and never sharing them with anyone. But she was, at the same time, terribly worried that Dennis would think ill of her for the choices she had made.

Sunny had resolved that she would enjoy this long weekend with Dennis and then she would reveal herself to him in good time.

As it turned out, the weekend was everything they had hoped it would be. They proved Dennis' theory about silences. They actually talked very little. They spent more time holding hands and watching romantic comedies, which they both loved, and smiling at each other over dinner and a glass of wine.

They sat in front of her ample fireplace and Sunny reread Dennis' letters to her out loud and they both laughed at his wit and he enjoyed watching her reactions to his words. They communicated with their eyes and their hands and their hearts. And on his last night in Okanogan, Sunny joined Dennis in the guest bed and they made love.

In that moment they were irrevocably joined. They could only go forward from here and they both reveled in the joy and the newness of it. How lucky they were to have found each other at last.

Leah had no school for the last two weeks of December,

but her job demanded a good deal of her time anyway. She had been assigned to a *pro bono* case at the end of November that both captivated her and consumed every minute she was at SeaYA.

The client was a girl of fifteen whose whole family had been killed in a house fire when she was just five. She had been the sole survivor among her parents and her two brothers and a sister. And she had been burned on over fifty percent of her body, including severe damage to her arms and face.

The girl's foster family had been allowed to adopt her. They received Social Security checks and disability payments through the State to care for her. Only they didn't care for her. Her condition required surgeries for skin grafts and laser treatments. Somehow the family claimed money for these procedures, but they were never done.

The pain and disfigurement from her injuries required that the girl be schooled at home. She was kept out of the eyes of society and held prisoner in her home for the money that could be gained in her name. It took seven long years before the girl figured out what her adoptive parents were up to. She overheard them one night talking about a check they were going to receive from the State and what they were going to spend it on.

She waited until they went out for an evening and she started snooping through their office, not quite knowing what she was looking for. What she found was that her parents, a psychiatrist and a mental health counselor, upstanding members of Seattle society, had been stealing from her for years. They had been manufacturing medical documents, claiming to have gotten treatments and surgeries for the girl that she never received.

She was twelve when the truth was revealed. There was a copy center right down the street from their downtown apartment. She had spent three years meticulously documenting the crimes of her adoptive parents in small increments and she had endured unimaginable pain and suffering while doing so, having never been treated for her devastating injuries.

She wanted more than criminal retribution for the injustice she had endured. The girl had done her homework. She'd paid her dues. She planned to publicly humiliate and expose her parents. And then she wanted her money back. When the time came, she fled to SeaYA for help, knowing that they could give the resources she needed to do just that.

Her name was Callie Justice and, as far as Leah was concerned, the girl had lived through hell and she was finally going to see redemption if it killed Leah and the rest of the *pro bono* department. Seattle Youth Alliance had given her a safe place to live and access to medical treatment and they were going after Dr. Cyrus Justice and Constance Justice with both guns blazing.

Leah loved the excitement of the case—the gathering of evidence, the pre-trial motions and affidavits and depositions, and the good that their organization was doing for one very unfortunate, but determined child. They would go to trial in May, barring any complications to the case.

SeaYA was in the news and so was Callie. Leah had to interview Callie several times and the two of them developed a quick friendship. Callie would have been beautiful if you could have only seen the left side of her face. She had hair long and straight and black as night and cat-shaped green eyes. She was a little plump from her lack of activity and the steroids she had to take to prevent rejection of her new skin grafts.

But she was one of the bravest individuals Leah had ever met and she admired Callie a great deal. They were going to win this case. They had to. She put in as many extra hours outside of school as she could and she visited Callie weekly to apprise her of their progress.

Working with Callie did make Leah think quite a bit about adoption and abandonment issues. She knew that she had been adopted when she was almost a year old. She had been so fortunate to have Shirley and Eileen. They doted on her and they loved her absolutely and unconditionally.

She couldn't imagine what would have happened to her had she been less lucky. It was a funny thing about Leah. Most adopted children wonder about their natural parents and their biology and many eventually seek the individuals that birthed them.

Leah never wondered about her biological mother. She remembered a conversation with Shirley when she was about six, when Shirley had volunteered to tell her about her mom and answer any questions she might have.

Leah couldn't think of anything to ask. Shirley volunteered that her mother had loved her very much and had wanted for her to be raised in a stable, loving home. She and Eileen had known her mother quite well, in fact. They had never expected to be blessed enough to raise

Leah. They had lost their first child to cancer, Leah's brother Garrett. They had never dreamed they would get to experience the joy of having another child.

Leah had been unnaturally curious about Garrett. She had wanted to know everything about her long-lost sibling, from his favorite foods and toys to his favorite books and animals. She had asked about everything—how he smelled, who he looked like, what he most enjoyed laughing about.

But she had never asked about her mother. It worried Eileen and Shirley endlessly, but in the end they figured it was because they were both mothers enough to keep her mind occupied well beyond simple biology. They just continued to nurture her and offer the truth if she ever sought it. They just went on with their lives, mostly forgetting that Sunny ever existed.

Chapter Twenty-eight

Sister Ellen grew increasingly weary as the winter turned to spring. She watched the emergence of the spring bulbs on the campus below from her dormitory window. She didn't know when her time would come, but she figured that God would give her a sign that it was coming.

After missing his November and December lunches with Sister Ellen, Dennis refused to miss any more. He was increasingly concerned about his old friend. She would not disclose just how ill she was, but her coloring was pale, her skin almost translucent, and she never left her living quarters. She also tired very quickly and ate very little of the pizza he now brought with him.

He also now knew about the full-time nurse. Sister Ellen had advised her nurse to remain scarce when visitors were there, but she had been forced to call on her a few times during Dennis' visits. He pressed her for more information, but she remained vague when asked questions about her health.

He brought news with him in February. Sunny had agreed to come and spend Easter and her spring break in April at his home in Seattle. Sister Ellen was thrilled for him. He seemed truly happy for the first time since he'd lost his Shelby. She didn't even think of disclosing what she knew about Sunny to him. They both deserved to be happy and Sunny certainly deserved to tell her own story when the time came. She only hoped that she would get to see the girl again. After all, Sister had been profoundly affected by their friendship and parting.

Leah dropped by on occasion to cheer Sister Ellen up. She was not young or naïve enough to think that Sister was getting better. She would pop by with a book from *Fat Cat Tales* or a Chai Tea from the Student Union Building and offer conversation and information about her goings-on.

Sister was bolstered just by the whoosh of strawberry-scented red hair as she gave her a quick hug and the sparkle in her eyes as she talked about the good work she was doing downtown. She loved her Leah. She was spending her last weeks and months making sure that Leah would realize just how much when she died.

Avery Moss dropped by Leah's cubicle on a late March afternoon. He had heard about her extra special efforts on behalf of Callie Justice. The entire *pro bono* department and her supervisor Lenny were impressed by her dedication and ability to solicit much-needed information from their client.

"Good afternoon, Leah," Avery began.

"Oh, hi, Mr. Moss. What a surprise!" Leah was trying to reorganize the entire Justice file before the case went to trial so she was buried up to her armpits in legal papers and depositions. She wanted so much at that moment to look cool and collected as the big boss showed up, but that was

228

impossible at the moment.

"You can call me Avery, Leah. I figure that we'll be working closely enough to use first names soon. That's why I'm here."

"I don't understand."

"I'd like to offer you a job when you graduate, Leah. That's in June, am I right?"

Leah was astounded. This was her first bona fide job offer!

"Yes, June. I've been getting my resume together, planning to send it to San Francisco, where my mom's are from, and to put out a few feelers here in Seattle too."

"Would you like to work for Seattle Youth Alliance?"

"I have enjoyed working here very much," then knowing that she had to play all of her cards, Leah said, "Of course, I would have to consider whatever offer you made and compare it to any others."

Avery smiled, admiring her gumption. She was an excellent student, he had checked and she probably would be made some sweet offers for employment upon graduation. He planned to trump them, though. An intern this bright did not come along very often.

"I will present you with a formal offer by mid-April, how does that sound? That'll give you time to get your applications out and get an idea where you might be headed. I just want you to know that I would be really proud to have you as part of our legal team."

"I am honored, Avery," she felt odd using his first name. "I'll look forward to seeing your offer."

"Have a good evening, Leah."

"Thanks. You too."

As he left, Leah let out the breath she'd been holding and gave a silent 'whoop,' throwing her arms in the air and stomping her feet. She'd just gotten her first real job offer and it was at a place she would love to work. She couldn't wait to go home and tell her moms!

Shirley and Eileen were ecstatic for Leah. Not only did she get a job offer—it was at a place they knew she enjoyed working and it was in *Seattle*. They had both been secretly terrified that she would be leaving as soon as she graduated.

She had talked about going to San Francisco for a few years now. They had visited several times when she was younger. It seemed almost like she could connect to her brother more by seeing his favorite places. Also, she loved the hustle of the larger city. There were many more job opportunities in the Bay area than in Seattle.

She still vowed to apply for Bay area jobs because she wanted to see what kind of an offer she could get, but Leah was completely wowed by Avery Moss' offering her a job so soon.

In a way, Leah wanted to stay close to the bookstore and Capitol Hill. She had spent her whole life here and her closest friends and most favorite places were here in Seattle.

But part of her wanted to break away. San Francisco was so exciting. It was hip and unconventional and progressive. But it would take a heck of an awesome job there to tear her away now.

When she got through giving Shirley and Eileen the

good news and they had fed her a celebratory meal at *Shuttle Burger* (complete with chocolate colas and wet fries,) Leah rushed over to give Sister Ellen the news before she went to bed, which she did so early these days.

Sister Ellen tried to match Leah's enthusiasm. After all, this would keep her close to Shirley and Eileen, which she was sure they were happy about. But she knew in her heart that she wouldn't be around to appreciate Leah's presence here.

The other trouble was this: Avery Moss was Sunny Moss' brother. Sunny Moss was in cahoots with Dennis Fulton, Avery's friend and second man at SeaYA. If Leah Kaye Foster Westfield was working there too, just how long could it be before everybody figured out who everybody else was?

Perhaps it was because she was burdened by all of these secrets that she worried so much. They might never know what she did. But she didn't want Leah's first place of employment to be a potential time bomb. Maybe it would be best if she went to San Francisco to avoid a mess.

She chose her response carefully.

"That is wonderful news, Leah. You should be so proud to get an offer from them so soon. You must be an impressive intern indeed!"

"I've really poured myself into this most recent case. And I love it there as well."

"Do you think it might be too safe of a choice for you, though, dear?"

"What do you mean by 'safe?'" Leah loved this wise old woman and she valued her opinion over almost anyone's.

"Well if you take a job at SeaYA, you would be living near where you've always lived, working at a place that you've already worked at, hanging out with the same people you've always known, going to the places that are as familiar to you as your own bedroom.

"There's nothing new or adventurous about choosing to take this job. Do you see what I mean?"

"I do, Sister Ellen. You're right. But there is something nice about familiarity too. Something comforting."

"I have to agree with you, dear. After all, look at me. I've been here forever, haven't I? I'm as much a creature of habit as there ever was! Who am I to talk?"

"You know I love your advice, Sister Ellen. You always tell me the truth. That's why I couldn't wait to tell you. You've given me something very valuable to think about."

"I am so proud of you, Leah, dear. You have become a fine young woman. Your mothers have done the best job. I know you'll make the right decision for yourself. I trust you to do that, Leah."

Leah hugged her old friend and wiped away the tears on both of their cheeks. This woman was as close to a grandmother as Leah had ever had and she said a small prayer for wellness for Sister Ellen as she pulled away.

"I have to go and let you get some rest. I love you, Sister Ellen."

"And I love you too, dear. You go have some good dreams tonight. Let them guide you."

"Sweet dreams to you, too, Sister Ellen." With that, she blew her a kiss and took her leave.

Chapter Twenty-nine

The letters arrived on the Saturday before Easter. Sister
Ellen had them delivered post haste by the resident assistant
from her floor of the residence hall. She had dreamed
of angels the night before. They had been unspeakably
beautiful, singing music that could only come from the
heavens.

God was telling her that her time was near. She needed
to see them all, everyone who mattered, whose secrets her
heart had kept. She wanted them all at once. So when she
woke up Saturday morning, fresh from the arms of the
angels, she wrote the letters.

The first arrived at noon at Dennis Fulton's West Seattle
beach house. Sunny was making lunch in the kitchen when
she heard the doorbell. She took the letter from the college
student at the door and took it straight to Dennis, who was
watching baseball in the den. It was lovely card stock with
an old-fashioned wax seal with a script letter 'R' on it.

She was curious as she handed him the letter, so she
stayed while he opened it. It read simply:

Dearest Dennis:

The arms of the Lord are reaching for me today. As you know, I have been ill and I am ready to succumb to whatever God has in store for me. I have just one wish and that is to see you—all of you. Please join me Easter morning. I will be in my finery, expecting you at 10 o'clock sharp.

Bring Sunny.

Do have a lovely day.

Yours forever,

Sister Ellen Ryan

Sunny recoiled. She knew that Dennis had a close friend who was a nun, but she never imagined, nor had she ever asked if that friend could be Sister Ellen!

She kept her surprise to herself as she comforted Dennis, who was obviously shaken that Sister Ellen had just admitted that she was dying. He had suspected as much, but it truly looked like tomorrow may be the last time he would see her. His sorrow was palpable.

Sunny would see him through this. He needed her. He had lost far too many women in his life—first his mom, then his wife, now Sister Ellen. Besides, she now knew that Sister Ellen had put the pieces together about her in Dennis' life. Sunny was mildly curious what the old lady had in mind for her tomorrow.

She, herself, had once loved and trusted Sister Ellen more than anyone and the nun had kept her secret all of these years. She owed it to her to go tomorrow even if it took risking everything she had built with this wonderful man.

Eileen and Shirley got their letter next at shortly after one o'clock. Business was in full-swing, as it usually was on a Saturday, but they left the counter to one of their employees and sat on a center sofa together as they saw Sister Ellen's signature wax monogram on the letter. They knew she'd been ill. They hoped this wasn't bad news. Their letter read:

To My Dears Eileen and Shirley:
Mothering is such a natural thing, but so difficult sometimes to do. You have nurtured the most wonderful child, you two, and I want you to know that it is because of this that I am asking you to come tomorrow. You have been dear friends and loving parents to Leah. I apologize now for any pain that my parting may bring to you, but my soul needs to have it this way. I know that you will understand.
I will be awaiting your visit tomorrow morning. Kindly arrive by ten o'clock sharp. You shall be the bells of my Easter ball.
Your true and loving friend,
Sister Ellen Ryan

They looked at each other strangely. What a cryptic message! They'd known Sister Ellen for the better part of thirty years. By all accounts, it looked like she was planning to die on them.

They mulled it over for a while, each trying to understand why she would be apologizing to them for doing so. She had been so ill the last several months. They didn't expect her to live forever.

Both were sad as they considered saying goodbye to their old friend. It was not going to be easy, but they would be there for her no matter what. She had always done the same for them.

Leah, was, as she had been in her spare time for most of the last two months, at SeaYA, working on the Justice case. Shirley and Eileen had directed the messenger of the letters to the office with Leah's letter so that she would get it right away. She received her letter at about two o'clock.

She also recognized Sister's wax stamp. She had always loved the personal touch this added to Sister's correspondence and she thought sometimes that Sister would write her letters just so that she could use her stamp, since she most certainly could have just stopped by to impart news of any kind.

The fact that this letter was delivered to her workplace, however, had Leah seriously worried. She sat down at her desk and unsealed the letter. It read:

To My Darling Leah:
Have you ever heard angels sing? I got to hear them in my dream last night. They're coming for me, dear, and they have voices sweeter than the lollipop we bought all those years ago.

I have one last gift for you, Leah, and I hope that you will understand and accept it for what it is. I need you to join me for Easter Sunday. Kindly be here at ten o'clock

sharp. I'll be dressed for the part, so wear ruffles and lace
if you desire. You always did when you were little.

I love you so much, darling, and I look forward to seeing
you tomorrow.

Yours forever and ever,
Sister Ellen Ryan

Tears sprung to Leah's eyes. She didn't think she could bear losing Sister Ellen. How in the world was she just supposed to put on a brave face and a fancy dress and go say goodbye to one of her dearest friends and confidantes? Sometimes Leah just wanted to be a little girl again, protected from all of the bad things in the world. Dying was bad, terrible, and she didn't want to face it.

But as she sat there and thought about it, she realized that Sister Ellen wouldn't mind dying at all. She had never known another individual with as much faith in God and heaven as Sister Ellen. She imagined that her passing would be very peaceful indeed as she went into God's willing arms.

She would just have to grow up and be there for her friend. She could face this. She just hoped her moms would be there with her so she could be their little girl again afterward.

Chapter Thirty

Easter Sunday had been rainy for the last ten years in
Seattle, making for soggy Easter egg hunts and soggier
kids. Not this year, though. This Easter dawned with clear
blue skies and unseasonably warm sunshine. The azaleas
were in their full glory and Sister Ellen admired them from
far above as she prepared for her special morning.

She had become accustomed to sleeping until nine
or ten, getting the extra rest that her failing body was
demanding. This morning, however, her mind and body had
been as sharp at six a.m. as they were in her thirties. She
helped herself to a long bath, asking the nurse to leave her
as she reveled in the sweet pear smell of her bath salts.

She combed her completely gray hair, which she had
allowed to grow long since she'd been confined to her
apartment. Then she pulled it back into a low bun at the
nape of her neck and proceeded to dress in her deep blue
Nun's Habit. It was the finest outfit she could think of to
wear on the day of Jesus' resurrection.

Leah would be disappointed that it had no frills or
lace, but that just couldn't be helped. She smiled as she
remembered how the little girl had loved to dress up for
Easter every year. Yellow had been her favorite color.

Sister Ellen called Father Milton to her room at precisely

eight-thirty and asked him to administer her last rites. He objected, saying she seemed in better health than she had in a while. She admonished him, telling him that only she and God knew better. He looked sad as he complied with her wishes.

It was shortly after nine-thirty by the time everything was in order for her guests. She decided to spend the spare time she had by sitting out on her balcony. If she faced the West side of the balcony, she could see sparkly blue Puget Sound. From the East she could see her beloved University campus. She spent a little bit of time examining both.

By the time ten o'clock arrived, Sister was waning. She had decided to receive her guests from her adjustable hospital bed, anyway, so she went ahead and lay down on top of her ivory eyelet bedding.

The mantel clock chimed ten o'clock and she heard the doorbell ring at precisely the same time. That would be Dennis. He was always right on time, never early, never late. She hoped he had convinced Sunny to come along.

The nurse led Dennis and Sunny to Sister's bedroom.

"Hello, Sunny, dear. So nice to see you again."

Tears welled up in Sunny's eyes both in pleasure at seeing the nun again and in sorrow that Sister Ellen looked so frail and pale and tiny in her great big habit. She looked nothing like the radiant, ethereal woman she had left twenty-five years ago. She looked vulnerable, mortal. Sunny realized how much she had missed her.

Dennis was puzzled. First of all, he hadn't expected Sister Ellen to be in her nun costume, as he called it. Second of all, it seemed like Sister knew Sunny. How could that be?

"Do you two know each other?"

"Dennis, darling, could you be a dear and fetch me a glass of water? I'm all worn out from my preparations this morning!"

He knew darn well that she could have asked her nurse to get the water for her, but he also knew when Sister was evading a question. He left them as Sister and Sunny joined hands.

"I've been praying since yesterday that you would allow Dennis to bring you. He doesn't need to know why, not from me, dear. I just wanted to give you one last gift before I take my leave."

With that, the doorbell rang again and the nurse led Eileen and Shirley and Leah into the room. Silence reigned supreme as the older women all looked at one another. Dennis came in with the glass of water and handed it to Sister, stymied by the electricity bolting between all of these women.

Leah had no clue. Her gaze focused on Sister Ellen, calmly sipping her water, and she dropped to her knees next to the bed. "You look beautiful, Sister Ellen. I always loved that shade of blue on you."

"That's so sweet of you, Leah Kaye," she looked pointedly at Sunny as she said her name. Suddenly she sounded short of breath as she started to give instructions. Her once commanding voice was weak and they strained to hear her. "Give me a hug, sweetheart. You're all here now and I am ready to go," she rasped.

"I need you all to do something for me. This may seem

a little dramatic, but I would like you all to stand in a circle around me, holding hands. First you, Sunny. Please hold my hand. Sunny, this is Leah. Leah, this is Sunny. Please hold each other's hands for me."

Eileen and Shirley looked at each other, alarmed and confused.

"Shirley and Eileen, can you please stand next to Leah? And Eileen, this is Dennis, also a dear friend of mine. Dennis, this is Eileen. Will you two please hold hands also?"

Sister's voice was almost a whisper by now. She took Dennis' hand. "I want you to all know that I love you. You have all touched my life immeasurably and you are all intertwined, perhaps because of me, more than you'll know. Thank you all for being here as I greet my angels. They're here, you know. Right behind you...."

Tears ran freely as they watched Sister Ellen's gaze go from each of their faces to an invisible space behind them. Her face lit up as if from within and she smiled and turned her eyes to the heavens. They were full of hope and joy, and then she closed them. The hands that had been holding Dennis' and Sunny's hands went suddenly limp.

Sister Ellen Ryan had gone into God's loving arms. Her nurse, who watched this all transpire from the doorway, wiped away her own tears and went to call Father Milton.

Dennis took Sister Ellen's hand and placed it and her other hand across her chest. He looked up to see how Sunny was doing and saw the raw sorrow painted across her pretty face. She lifted Leah's hand to her lips and kissed the back of it and then let it go. Leah nodded to her and then let loose the sobs that she had been holding back.

She fell into her mothers' waiting arms and took comfort there, as she always had. With a quick nod to Sunny, Eileen and Shirley escorted their heartbroken daughter out of the room.

Dennis was crestfallen, but glad that he had gotten to see Sister Ellen die with all of the dignity and grace she had displayed throughout her life.

Sunny walked over to him and into his waiting arms. "I need to tell you a story, my love. Let's go home."

Dennis leaned over and kissed Sister Ellen's cool forehead and then, knowing there was nothing else they could do, they went on their way.

Dennis' beach house had a sunken living room with a stunning view of Puget Sound and on this bright Easter day, it seemed like the right place for Sunny to tell her story.

She invited Dennis to sit next to her. He grabbed them each a soda from his mini-fridge while she started talk.

"I need to tell you about my last day in Seattle twenty-five long years ago. I've never told anyone this story, so you must know what it is costing me to do so. But it's long overdue and I trust you, Dennis. Here goes:

"Twenty-five long years ago, I was working as a waitress in a restaurant when my brother Avery found me. He was a law student at the time and very busy himself, but he was so happy to have found me that he made arrangements to take me home. I agreed to go with him, but I made him take me a few places first.

"My first stop was Sister Ellen's apartment, where we

242

just watched her die. I needed her guidance and, in a way, her forgiveness for what I was about to do. She gave it. She watched me walk away and, God help me, she still loved me after all of that." Sunny paused to hold back a sob and take a drink of her cold soda.

"My second stop was *Fat Cat Tales*. Are you familiar with it? Eileen and Shirley, whom you just met, are the owners of the store and the apartment above it. I asked Avery to wait for me in the car, yet again, and I went in. Eileen was minding the store.

"Shirley was up in the apartment playing with the most adorable little red-headed, blue-eyed cherub you ever did see. She was bribing the little girl with cheese puffs so that she would crawl toward her and pull herself up to get one.

"The baby was eleven months old and perfect in every way. Happy, well-adjusted, well-fed, and loved. She was mine, Dennis. My sweet Leah Kaye Moss. I was just holding her hand not a half-hour ago. She's all grown up. I swear it's like looking in a mirror seeing her! You just change out the hair and she's me sixteen short years ago. Did you see the resemblance?"

Dennis was mesmerized, "I didn't look for it, Sunny. Please…go on."

"I took her from Shirley, saying she needed her diaper changed, and took her into the room that she and I shared. You see, Eileen and Shirley saved my baby and I from the streets. We were living in a cellar on the side of an abandoned apartment building when Sister Ellen took me to them. By the time I left, Leah had become as attached to Shirley and Eileen as she was to me.

"I like to think that my motives were purely unselfish when I left Leah that day, Dennis, but to some extent, they were selfish. I was ready to act like the teenager that I was again. I wanted to go home and never have them know that I was a drug addict and a runaway and a teenage mother. And they never have known, have they? Would they still think of me the same way? I'm not sure.

"But what I told myself that day was that I was leaving Leah so that she could have a better life than I could give her. I was so messed up myself, how could I possibly be a good mother to her? How could I possibly give her good schools and nice clothes and healthy self-esteem, all of the things that Shirley and Eileen have given her?

"I could have given her my love, though, Dennis. If I had not been so proud, so selfish, so young, I could have just gone on giving her my love. I was a good mother—— you should have seen me." Sunny was crying openly now, grieving the loss she'd felt just as acutely twenty-five years ago. He handed her his handkerchief.

"So here's what I did: I didn't have a whole lot of time because Avery was outside waiting for me. I took Leah to my room and I told her how much I loved her, but that I would never be able to offer her anything other than that. I told her that Eileen and Shirley would be her substitute mommys and that she would just forget me someday. And then I just held her for the longest time, memorizing how she felt and how she smelled and how her little red whale spout pigtail tickled my chin. I kissed each of her fingers and her toes. I traced the outline of her lips with my pinky finger, loving how she broke into a pout as I did so.

244

"And then I kissed her eyes, feeling each eyelash flutter in surprise at the sensation. And then I changed her diaper and put her in a fresh pair of jammies, just so that I could know how it felt to dress her just one last time. And I memorized her features, Dennis. She was impossibly beautiful, just the slightest blush to her cheeks and the happiest, most curious sparkle to her clear blue eyes.

"I can't tell you how many times I have wanted to paint that face. But I haven't. It's just printed on every memory that I have.

"I put Leah in her crib, then and penned a quick note to Eileen and Shirley, explaining that I was leaving and that I wanted them to raise Leah, because I knew they would be wonderful parents. I had heard so many stories about their sweet, little boy Garrett, who had died of cancer. In a way, I wanted to give them my child to make up for the loss that they had experienced.

"But then there I go trying to sound all selfless and benevolent again about abandoning my child. I could have chosen differently. I know that now. But that stupid kid left that perfect little girl behind in her crib with her completely inadequate note taped to it. And then I grabbed my paintbrushes and a few other personal things and bolted out the door and never looked back."

Sunny, spent from recalling the agony of saying goodbye to her child, simply stopped talking and waited for Dennis' reaction.

What he did surprised and amazed her. He simply enfolded her in his arms and cried with her. They cried for the young teenager who felt compelled by poverty and inadequacy to leave her own child. And they cried for Sister Ellen who held this precious secret from Leah and Dennis clear to her deathbed. And they took comfort from each other.

When they were both quiet and calm again, Sunny told Dennis everything else. All of the stories and experiences she'd had during her years away—she finally shared them all. She told him about Raymond's complete rejection of her. She told him about living in an unheated, rat-infested cellar for eight months. She told him about her drug addiction—the weakness and stupidity of that life. She even told him she believed it was her fault that her grandmother had gotten hurt.

He continued to kiss away her tears and then when she was quiet again, he took her to bed and made slow, sweet love to the brave woman who had shared everything possible with him. This would bind Sunny to him forever. And in the morning, he was going to ask her to marry him too.

Chapter Thirty-one

The news of Sister Ellen's passing spread like wildfire across campus and then citywide. She was a beloved figure in Seattle from her stint as a radio personality to role as a spiritual mentor to several generations of Seattle University students, men and women alike.

Her funeral mass was held at the Chapel of St. Ignatius on campus. The planners knew that the venue would not be nearly large enough for her mourners, so they projected a speaker outside and placed chairs stretching both directions clear over to the Piggott Building. The spiritual community at Seattle University just knew that Sister Ellen would have wanted to be mourned in this place she loved so much.

Every inch of the allotted space was packed with mourners. It was a beautiful, simple mass, and Sister Ellen looked truly ethereal in her deep blue habit inside her gilded coffin. She would have enjoyed all of the pomp and circumstance of the lovely spring day. They felt her there in spirit at the reception in the Campion Ballroom later.

Several of her coworkers got up to share Sister Ellen stories and to impart what she had told them about their futures via their palm readings or their dreams. The atmosphere was sad, but celebratory at the same time.

After it was all over, Leah took herself to Sister Ellen's

room. She had left no will, so to speak, but she, in true Sister Ellen style, had left little yellow sticky notes on everything that she wanted to go to certain people. She thought it much more efficient than that whole lawyer and will-reading thing.

Leah had been left all of Sister's scrapbooks. There must have been at least twenty of them, but according to her nurse, she had finished them all over the winter months, not wanting her work to be incomplete. She packed the books into Eileen's car and on her last trip grabbed the painted stones that Sister had left one each to Eileen and Shirley. She would take them by on her way to the office. They were curious little things, but very pretty, with a kale plant painted on each one.

She put them on the passenger seat next to her. Then she bid adieu to the residence hall where she had spent so much time with her dear friend, Sister Ellen. She didn't think she'd probably ever ride that elevator again. She said a silent and tearful goodbye.

She stopped by *Fat Cat Tales* and then went on to the office. The trial was in just three weeks and the whole legal department was abuzz with the work that would have to be done beforehand. Leah was able to lose herself in her work.

It would be the middle of June after their successful trial against the Justice parents and graduation before Leah would get around to looking through Sister Ellen's scrapbooks. Sister had neatly labeled them by volume. She put a personal letter for Leah at the beginning of the first volume. It said:

Dearest Leah Kaye:

If you are reading this letter, then I have finally passed into the arms of the Lord. By the Grace of God, hopefully you were with me at the time. I know I would have hated to be alone.

It has taken many painstaking moments to preserve my many secrets. The burden of being a nun is that you take the secrets of a woman's heart, which every woman has anyway, and you add to them the secrets told to you under the most discreet and confidential circumstances. It wears on you after a while, as I'm sure you will learn during your legal career where you will do very much the same thing.

I want you to find your own way to the secrets of your life. Perhaps you don't want to know the truth of your birth. But there are a few things that I want to unburden myself of because you have to know the miracle that you are to me.

I never told you, Leah, but I knew your biological mother, quite well actually. When you came into this world, Leah, dear, it was my hands that caught you. I had found your mother living in a dark, dank, rodent-laden cellar. The Lord had led me deliberately to her via my dreams. You know how much I relied on those!

But anyway, I found her in the advanced stages of labor and with no one around to help us, your mother and I made do. She pushed you out so bravely and I rather ineptly caught you! I acted like I knew what I was doing, but it was all very frightening and happened very quickly. The truth is that I felt responsible for you from that moment on, Leah. I never birthed a child, but you were much like a grandchild to me. And I loved you very, very much.

I led you and your mother to Shirley and Eileen. You were almost a year old when your mother decided to leave and I gave her my blessing. I hope that doesn't upset you, Leah, that I let your mother off the hook for leaving you, but I believe that she did it with every good intention, for herself and for you, darling. Just look at how well your mothers have raised you. I made certain of it.

I've also heard that your mother made quite of a success of herself. I found that out by accident. A good friend of mine is in love with her, you see and it sounds like she did well with the opportunity to get an education. I know that her decision to leave you was not easy for her, but I am glad to know that both of you have done so well despite doing so apart from each other.

This is all I have to say. You are going to see some of my meager attempts at drawing in these pages, as well as photographs from my younger days and from my early days as a nun and at the University. You have my pictorial history of my life in your hands, Leah, and I hope it will tell the story and that it may be my legacy.

Or perhaps I should revise that. Perhaps you are my legacy, beautiful Leah. Because aside from giving my life to serve God, apart from taking my vows, the single most significant event in my life was watching you come into this world. You are the future, and the light of so many lives, Leah. May God be with you as you begin your journey.

With all of my love and faith—
Sister Ellen Ryan

Leah couldn't see through her tears to continue at that point, so she had lunch downstairs at the counter with her moms. They talked about the job she had taken in San Francisco and the trip they were going to take in July to go apartment hunting. They had a few contacts left down there that would hook her up with a good place.

They discussed whether to give her Eileen's car and buy a new one for themselves or to buy Leah a newer, more economical car which she would assume the payments for once she got on her feet.

Leah enjoyed every minute of the conversation. Sure her moms were sad to see her spread her wings, but they were as excited as she that she was going to have this adventure. They were proud of her for making the tough decision not to stay at SeaYA. Instead, she was going to be an assistant to the District Attorney, sticking her smarts to criminal law for at least a short while. She would be poor, but she would be fighting the good fight.

Leah left the bookstore with a good feeling and the readiness to dive into Sister Ellen's past. It was late into the night when Leah opened the seventh volume. Her eyes were tired, but she was enjoying herself immensely. Sister Ellen had been a gloriously complicated woman, all about fun and her faith.

She turned the fifth page of the volume and froze. There was an uncannily real sketch of herself when she was about seven holding a lollipop. Come to think of it, she remembered that lollipop. She enjoyed the sketch of herself, but it was the one across from it that really got her attention.

If you added about ten pounds to her frame, the sketch could have been Leah, but the hair was different. This was a close-up and you could almost tell that the eyes were blue, though it was a black and white sketch. This wasn't Leah, this she knew for certain. It was her mother.

She looked below the picture where Sister Ellen had simply scripted, 'Sunny.'

Her mind locked the pieces of the puzzle into place. The woman named Sunny who was engaged to and marrying Mr. Fulton later that summer, the woman who was Avery Moss' sister, the woman who had held her hand and Sister Ellen's as she had died, the woman who had so strangely kissed the back of her hand before she let it go—that was her biological mother.

The tremor of shock came over her and then went again. She had actually held her mother's hand. But then she remembered definitely that upon letting go of that hand, she had gone straight into her *real* mothers' arms.

And that was where she always would be. Despite biology, Leah Kaye was Shirley and Eileen's daughter. She was glad, however, that Sister Ellen had connected the dots for her. It was one less mystery to solve.

Life was waiting for Leah to live it. Sunny gave it to her to begin with. Eileen and Shirley nurtured it. Sister Ellen watched it grow. And now she was on her way, despite, or perhaps, *because* of all of it.

She closed the volume quietly and turned off her light to go to sleep. She had a lifetime to study Sister Ellen. The question was—what would she do in the meantime?

Kimberly Ann Freel

Kimberly Ann Freel was born and raised in rural Okanogan County. She was educated at Seattle University with a major in Diagnostic Ultrasound. After working in the medical field for over 10 years, Kimberly decided to pursue her passion for writing. *Painted Rocks* is her debut novel.

Kimberly is an avid reader and enjoys gardening, crafting, and spending time with her family. She and her husband and their children live on a ranch outside of Okanogan, Washington, where she has finished her second novel and is currently at work on a third.

Contact Information
Youth and Adults who may need or want services feel free to contact these organizations

YouthCare-Serving At-Risk and Homeless Youth Since 1974
www.youthcare.org   24-Hour Crisis Line: **800.495.7802**

Address:2500 NE 54th St.
　　　　Seattle, WA 98105
Phone: 206.694.4500
Fax: 206.694.4509
Other: 800.833.6388

Mailing List & General Info:
Lisa.Govro@youthcare.org
Donations:
Lisa.Govro@youthcare.org
206.694.4500 ext. 1223

Okanogan Family Planning
All services are confidential and non-judgmental.
Sliding fee scale available. Most services are free for teens.
509.422.1624 / 800.660.1624
www.okanoganfamilyplanning.org
127 Juniper Street North
Omak, Washington 98841

Okanogan County Support Center
To break the cycle of violence,
We must break the cycle of silence.
509.826.3221 / 1.888.826.3221

Made in the USA